FRESH BLOOD

FRESH BLOOD
New Canadian Gothic Fiction

edited by

ERIC HENDERSON & MADELINE SONIK

Fresh Blood
copyright © 1998 The Authors

published by Ravenstone
an imprint of Turnstone Press
607 – 100 Arthur Street
Artspace Building
Winnipeg, Manitoba
R3B 1H3 Canada
www.TurnstonePress.com

All rights reserved. No part of this book may be reproduced or transmitted in any form or by any means—graphic, electronic or mechanical—without the prior written permission of the publisher. Any request to photocopy any part of this book shall be directed in writing to the Canadian Copyright Licensing Agency, Toronto.

Turnstone Press gratefully acknowledges the assistance of the Canada Council for the Arts, the Manitoba Arts Council and the Government of Canada through the Book Publishing Industry Development Program for our publishing activities.

"Cerberus" from *Cerberus* (1993) by Rai Berzins used by permission of Goose Lane Press. "Evil Eye" from *Evil Eye* (1994) used by permission of Véhicule Press. "The Last Ferry" from *Sleeping with the Insane* (1995) used by permission of Goose Lane Press. Some of these stories have appeared in *Canadian Fiction Magazine*, *Event*, *The Fiddlehead*, *Grain*, *The Malahat Review*, and *Prism International*.

Original cover photograph by Michael P. Callaghan
Author photograph by Michael Tourigny
Design: Manuela Dias

This book was printed and bound in Canada
by Printcrafters for Turnstone Press.

Canadian Cataloguing in Publication Data

Fresh blood: new Canadian gothic fiction

ISBN 0-88801-228-4

1. Fantastic fiction, Canadian (English).*
2. Short stories, Canadian (English).*
I. Henderson, Eric, 1957–   II. Sonik, Madeline, 1960–

PS8323.F3 F74 1998   C813'.0872908054
PR9197.35.F35 F74 1998   C98-920163-5

Contents

Introduction ..../1

Into the Places of Those Lost .... /11
    Kenneth J. Harvey

The Story of an Eye...................... /25
    Norman Ravvin

These Are Ghost Stories .... /31
    Elyse Gasco

The Last Ferry.......................... /53
    Jennifer Mitton

Letters (On a Book Lately Circulating in the
Offices of Transport Canada)................ /69
    André Alexis

Cerberus .... /85
    Rai Berzins

The Beautiful Children .... /108
    Michael Kenyon

A Thin White Hand .... /118
    Kenneth J. Emberly

The Apostle............................ /132
    Madeline Sonik

Peterborough........................... /140
    Derek McCormack

Evil Eye .... /143
    Ann Diamond

Instructions for Navigating
the Labyrinth........................../156
    Méira Cook

Miasma................................/164
    Ernest Hekkanen

Torch ..../179
    Thea Caplan

Hounds ..../193
    Annabel Lyon

Contributors............................/201

Introduction
by Eric Henderson & Madeline Sonik

Before it was applied to writing, the "Gothic" referred to an ornate, often overwrought or "barbaric," style of architecture and art. The implications of primitivism and decadence carried over to the kind of fiction, written mostly in the late eighteenth and early nineteenth centuries, that expressed the fears and repressions lying behind the Classicist world view and institutions like the Catholic Church. The Gothic took its revenge on collective, seemingly stable, authoritarian structures by haunting their presumptive harmonies with threatening, ghostly presences and demonic subjugators.

In his 1962 study of contemporary writers, *New American Gothic*, Irving Malin employed the term "New Gothic," and although today it is used rather sporadically (and often interchangeably with "Gothic"), the literary New Gothic refers less to a precise form or style, or to specific content, and more to a tenebrous, alien sensitivity to the energies of the unconscious. The New Gothic has merged with our postmodern sensibilities to become a useful tool for exploring the uncertainties and contradictions of our world.

Americans, of course, have no unique claim on the Gothic or the New Gothic. Canadian fiction has its Gothic ancestor in John Richardson, Canada's first native-born novelist and author of the once-popular *Wacousta* (1832). According to Michael Hurley's recent study of Richardson's work, *The Borders of Nightmare*, Gothic novelists sustained Richardson in his efforts to "shock a garrison culture into an awareness of what a chamber of horrors its own smugly regarded world really is."[1]

Like American New Gothic, Canadian New Gothic has emerged with a dismaying lack of precision from a welter of past associations and present-day realities. Still, the stories collected in this volume share a common ground, being interrelated literarily and culturally.

Blood Lines

When most people speak of the Gothic today, they are alluding to the form practiced by the old Gothic writers, a form bristling with macabre associations: rattling suits of armor, mazy corridors in crumbling castles, innocent maidens offered on altars to the lurid pleasures of mad monks. Gothic novelists like Horace Walpole, whose 1765 *The Castle of Otranto* heralded this innovative and exotic fictional form, along with Ann Radcliffe, Mary Shelley, and several others whose works today are seldom read, never cared much for critical acceptance, but were satisfied to present themselves essentially as entertainers. That their inferior imitators tried to do nothing more challenging than manipulate their readers' emotions using as their apparatus a limited range of stylized and ready-made Gothic effects hardly enhanced the literary reputation of the Gothic. Replaying the same tired scenarios before a dwindling readership led to death by cliché of the Gothic novel: the old form cracked and broke asunder around 1820, but from this wreckage, what wonders!

No doubt influenced both by the former popularity of the Gothic and by its intuited truths, many Victorian novelists, like Charles Dickens, George Eliot, and the Brontë sisters, sought to harness or channel the Gothic sensibility. But the Victorians were not really Gothicists by nature or inclination; lacking Nietzsche, Freud, and Jung, many took their cue from Ann Radcliffe, whose supernatural effects were explained away in her

INTRODUCTION

rational endings, and were more concerned with domesticating it. Whatever the case, the Gothic continued to exist cocoon-like, awaiting its next incarnation.

Many readers today are indebted to Edgar Allan Poe for the development of the detective and mystery genres. It was also Poe who located the center of Gothic angst within the psyche, where it can be found in today's New Gothic, in subversive (in)human drives and inexplicable motivations; Poe psychologized and individualized the Gothic, in effect recasting René Descartes's rationalistic formula, "I think, therefore I am," in terms more compatible with postmodernist thought: "I do not think, therefore I destroy."

The Gothic, then, is concerned with revealing the underside of human existence, but how it achieves its revelation of "otherness" is more open to speculation; a defining trait of the Gothic and the New Gothic is that they raise far more questions than they answer.

Blood Relations

Poe not only realigned the Gothic, but conjured a new genre from the ashes of the old: that of the murder mystery or detective story. The mystery, along with the related forms of the supernatural or ghost story, and the horror story, shares its ancestry with the literary New Gothic, though differing markedly in aim. In a sense, the murder mystery can be seen as the flip side of the New Gothic: in the former, the rules are set according to a covert writer-reader agreement and cannot be broken; the murder mystery proceeds from the unknown toward certitude, from mystery to discovery. The supernatural tale derives its energy from our willingness to suspend, without doing entirely away with, our logic and reason, while the horror story calls on the emotions of fear and horror in its direct evocation of human evil.

How does the New Gothic differ from these? As suggested,

the predictability of the murder mystery pattern is inimical to the New Gothic, which, in its very open-endedness, draws its life's breath by flouting or undermining reified structures of all kinds—institutional, social, familial, even narrational. The ghost story, ultimately, depends on our acceptance of our rationality, a belief that makes suspension of that belief possible. Finally, while both the horror story and the New Gothic assume humanity's irrationality, the horror story's level of appeal is to our visceral, feeling and sensing aspects. The New Gothic's appeal is more intellectual or philosophical; it analytically probes the roots of our behavior in our unconscious, repressed being. Its "literariness" derives partly from its seriousness. While a good New Gothic story entertains its readers, it does so more by challenging their assumptions than by fulfilling them.

Ties that Bind

Like a child who is dutiful yet independent, the New Gothic both acknowledges and downplays its heritage. Although the old Gothic did not eschew realism (once the premise of creating human life is accepted, *Frankenstein* becomes an amalgam of romance and realistic elements), it usually incorporated non-realistic, often supernatural, ingredients and dolorous atmospheric effects. Omens, family curses, ghostly visitations, timely thunderstorms have little relevance to the literary New Gothic, but continue to be played out in the popular ghost or horror story.

In two main areas the child resembles its parent. As mentioned, though the means used to frighten the reader have changed (in effect, today's New Gothic tends to disturb, rather than shock, to make its reader anxious, rather than fearful), the New Gothic remains committed to the dynamics of unconscious process and to an anti-authoritarian stance.

The second point of resemblance relates to character. During the time that the Gothic novel was popular, the Sentimental novel was a rival form; while Sentimental novelists tried to evoke a gush of tears for their victimized female characters, Gothic novelists tried to terrorize their readers by exaggerating the *predicament* of their (again, usually female) characters. Reader identification became crucial to the success of the Sentimental novel, but not of the Gothic novel, where too intense an identification would undermine the Gothic effect. It is with Poe's victims as with other characters in Gothic fiction: whether they are walled up, entombed, assaulted, or mutilated, we are more apt to respond to the horrors of their situation than to pity their suffering.

What has helped make the Gothic such a popular and enduring form is the directness of its appeal to its readers through characters that act as transparent screens beyond which, alarmingly, readers see themselves stripped of their defences and evasions. By various strategies the New Gothic writer leads us to examine searchingly the dark corners of our own psyches. The best New Gothic writing implicates us in some obscure but unmistakable collusion with its author in unraveling the puzzle of our baffling and unacknowledged selves. American Gothicist John Hawkes once alluded to the beneficial effects of "evil" in his works in making the reader "face up to the enormities of ugliness and potential failure within ourselves and in the world around us."[2] This could serve as the New Gothic writer's oath of office.

Dark Doings in the Cellar

In the late 1980s, two English anthologies of Quebec stories appeared: *Invisible Fictions* and *Intimate Strangers*. Their editors made a similar point in emphasizing the surreal, the grotesque, and the gothic qualities of contemporary Quebec fiction, qualities that, said editor Geoff Hancock, might surprise English readers, accustomed as they were to a more socially-oriented realism.[3] However, the easy dichotomy between anglophone and francophone Canadian short fiction has been challenged, most recently by Margaret Atwood.

In her book *Strange Things: The Malevolent North in Canadian Literature*, Atwood argues, as she has before, that behind the mask of English Canada's straightlaced traditionalism lies a buried life: "Boringness, in anglophone Canadian Literature, and even sometimes in its life, is often a disguise concealing dark doings in the cellar."[4] English Canadian Literature today is seldom boring, but Atwood's comment provokes the tantalizing hypothesis that while the Gothic strain emerges more openly in contemporary Quebec fiction, it is often resisted and suppressed by anglophone traditionalist consciousness, erupting through its literature nonetheless, but in a form that is often less conspicuously and self-consciously "gothic."

Though one can trace a line of descent in Canadian Gothic from the old Gothicists and their influence on Richardson to contemporary writers like W.O. Mitchell, Robertson Davies, Timothy Findley, Atwood, and several others, it is apparent that the Gothic is less a shaping force in our literature than it is in the American literary tradition of Poe, Hawthorne, and Melville. A clue to the mystery of our contemporary gothicity may well lurk not so much in our literary heritage as behind the Canadian obsession with national identity with its double threat of usurpation (Americanization) and fragmentation (regionalism).

Fears of economic (and by implication political) dominance gained rhetorical force in the 1960s and early '70s. The issue resurfaced with the impassioned debate over the Free Trade agreement with the United States in the late '80s. It may well be that the perceived collective threat to what we define as "Canadian" generates an archetypal Gothic terror in our national psyche, giving free rein in our literature to images of exploitation and domination. Interestingly, much of the debate over free trade focused on the consequences of such an accord on Canada's artistic integrity.

Today the threat may be less external, reflected rather in the

INTRODUCTION

instability of Canada's internal divisions. Whether the psyche is individual or collective, turning inward to introspective self-questioning, when conducted in a spirit of honesty and bravery, inevitably leads to an examination of our motivations and repressed desires and the consequent discovery of things about ourselves that are not particularly pleasing or reassuring. The implications inherent in the question of a Canadian identity often assume the threatening shape of those underground forces that act to undermine the fragile concept of an outer identity.

All this suggests—albeit more theoretically than empirically—that the Gothic sensibility has a reason to flourish in Canadian Literature in the '90s. That it *does* indeed flourish in recent short fiction is evinced by the stories in this volume. However, Canadian New Gothic is drastically under-represented in '90s anthologies of Gothic and New Gothic published outside Canada, while many editors of English Canadian anthologies still seem to favor more traditional forms of storytelling.

New Directions for the New Gothic

Early commentators noted the motif of female imprisonment and helplessness in Gothic novels. More recently, there has been much theorizing about the socio-cultural significance of female subjugation in literature. The challenging of patriarchal values and resultant instability of gender assumptions and definitions have had interesting ramifications on the New Gothic. It is now possible to reexamine the familiar Gothic motif of female captivity in light of newly emerging cultural values.

The New Gothic female character in anglophone Canadian fiction is seldom simply a passive vessel for male desire or domination. Much New Gothic fiction focuses on the ravages of a dark feminine consciousness, acknowledging a new-found female power to confound or destroy restrictive, masculine-centered systems. The wounded narrator of Ann Diamond's "Evil Eye" summons a catastrophic potency of her own against a demeaning husband, while in the unique vision that Elyse Gasco presents in "These Are Ghost Stories," domesticity is defamiliarized as a Gothic search for meaningful ritual.

A new male consciousness of confinement seems to be emerging in New Gothic stories. In Rai Berzins's word-haunted "Cerberus," for example, the narrator, while living an apparently "normal" life, descends to a personal hell cohabited by monsters and outcasts. In Kenneth J. Harvey's "Into the Places of Those Lost," a man's sexual fantasy becomes a frightening, hallucinatory embrace of what seems the ghost of his dead wife.

But the Gothic dynamic is by no means restricted to the masculine-feminine sphere; its informing voice, its probing essence, is tuned to the eerie vibrations of an inner shadowy self fraught with dangers to the ego and its clamorous neediness. This voice, neither specifically male nor female, is often heard in New Gothic fiction as it withdraws further from the claims of worldliness, sometimes beyond language into vacancies of silence, as in André Alexis's darkly satiric "Letters"; in Annabel Lyon's "Hounds," this voice resonates with a haunting austerity. Like the old Gothic with its subversive attitude toward the Age of Reason, the New Gothic derives much of its power and eloquence from a wayward spirit of rebelliousness, moving beyond convention to celebrate its own space.

The Gothic has always proven adaptable. With its radicalization as an agent for change, supporting new and divergent cultural vantages, the New Gothic has become an increasingly relevant literary form. The relation of Gothic writing to the society it both mirrors and critiques recalls D.H. Lawrence on Poe's writing. Answering the complaint of moralists on why Poe's tales need have been written, Lawrence argues:

> They need to be written because old things need to die and disintegrate, because the old white psyche has to be gradually broken down before anything else can come to pass.[5]

INTRODUCTION

The old Gothic novelists hardly thought of themselves as agents for change, as precursors of revitalized fictional forms. And yet, they were. It is tempting to speculate down what uncharted roads—fictional or cultural—the New Gothic is leading us.

NOTES

1. Michael Hurley, *The Borders of Nightmare: The Fiction of John Richardson* (Toronto, 1992), 18.
2. L.S. Dembo and Cyrena N. Pondrom, eds., *The Contemporary Writer: Interviews with Sixteen Novelists and Poets* (Madison, 1972), 6.
3. Geoff Hancock, ed., *Invisible Fictions: Contemporary Stories From Quebec* (Toronto, 1987), 9.
4. Margaret Atwood, *Strange Things: The Malevolent North in Canadian Literature* (Oxford, 1995), 64.
5. D.H. Lawrence, *Studies in Classic American Fiction* (New York, 1961), 65.

INTO THE PLACES OF THOSE LOST
by Kenneth J. Harvey

for Robert Rutherford

The bloodhound rushed to the side of the cabin, poking her nose beneath the garbage box lid and flicking it up, only to have it clunk down on her head. She barked and sniffed manically, pushing farther into the darkness, then jolting back an instant later, freezing on stiff legs as the raccoon leapt out. Running for twenty feet, with Sag in close pursuit, the raccoon stopped dead in its tracks, turning and lifting its tiny paws to the dog. Sag skidded to a halt, with a snort and a muddled "rhaaaa" sound that was more like a bad cough than a bark, before crouching low and backing off.

Cuz watched the scene with a smile on his swollen lips. He picked at his cheek, carefully pulling away a small piece of skin still coming off from the woodstove's flash fire that had rushed against his face, the wood being too dry, when he had been told that it was wet (wrongfully taking someone's word at face value), and he had laced the junks with gasoline to keep things going. One match, and his face changed with a furious roar licking his skin into a crumpled mess. Carefully, most times absent-mindedly, he peeled away the skin, feeling a freshness that soon made him think of laughter. He called to his wife with words concerning the raccoon chase, and Bridey looked up from the new red spinner she was fixing to her trouting pole, and came to the door with an even, reasonable expression, leaning out to watch. But the raccoon was gone, the bloodhound standing in the blueberry brush sadly staring back at the cabin, as if nothing less than her life had been taken away from her. Disappointment in herself and everything that had led her to that spot. Bridey could not help but laugh at the look on the bloodhound's face, glancing at Cuz before turning back into the house, not knowing, not seeing how she herself would be found dead in her car the next day, on her way home from working for the Highways Department on the road-widening project outside Cutland Junction, through with standing in the dust all day, feeling the heat and the gritty sweat beneath her hard hat, holding up the SLOW sign that was turned around in the palm of one hand, again and again, to the big white word against red—STOP.

Filling his duffel bag with one change of clothes, a few tins of stew and soup, a sleeping bag, and an ax, Cuz wandered off into the woods with Sag following close behind. The policeman had told him that his wife had died by accident, and Cuz had merely nodded his head, understanding what that meant. He climbed into the police car and was taken to the hospital that was, according to the green highway sign, twelve miles away in St. Shotts. The room where he had seen his wife was terribly bright and everything was made of cool silver, even the table she was lying on. The room smelled sharp and seemed to sting all the space inside his body. When the man pulled back the sheet, he saw it was his wife. The man moved the blanket down further to show Cuz that she was naked and seemingly unmarked, her flesh the wrong color—a polished greenish-white—but he needed it all the same, seeing her still and changed this way, feeling the final frightening rush of arousal that made him want to climb on top, thinking he could bring her back with his mouth and the warmth of his body and what he would let loose inside her after he fit between her legs the way he was meant to.

The sheet was slowly pulled back up, and Cuz looked to see the man with the brown-rimmed glasses nodding his head, then carefully slipping a black strand of hair, hanging down the side of the silver table, back under the white, shape-fitting blanket. Cuz stared at the man's hands, his fingernails, the white cleanness of them. He was startled by how the man stayed there with his wife when they left. Cuz glanced back and thought, "Wha' rights he 'av?" He jerked to get loose and say a thing or two to the man with the long white coat, but the policeman held his arm, saying confidently, "Come on, Cuz. She's gone now. Let's all of us try to be reasonable."

That evening, around dusk time, the raccoon came by again, lingering in the trees and watching, thinking it might be a trap because Cuz had dumped the garbage out of the bin at the side of the cabin, everything out from inside, to see what would come to claim the refuse, finding it necessary now for these things to be accepted by another. Both of his feet stepping and standing firmly in the dark rushing willfulness, his shaky limbs held defiantly stiff among the mad release of all that was tossed off and accepted into the wild order of more basic, but seemingly wiser creatures. Faith. God. Animals that must eat. And shit out the stuff of biological communion that makes this world grow greener.

Cuz watched from behind the wall of the cabin, leaning close to the small square window, and fingering the tufts of moss stuck into the spaces between the stacked logs that made up the walls, thinking of other things, the brittleness of Bridey's cunny hairs. The tangle that his fingers caught in, searching for wetness. The wetness gone, drought hardening the once sleek, fleshy, life-sucking hole.

Dead dry now, and black rubber hard.

The raccoon waddled closer, paying no attention to Sag lying fifteen feet away with her head resting on her outstretched paws. The raccoon approached the dog, but Sag only shuffled backward, mournfully slow, along the scratchy blueberry brush, not wanting to find fault in the presence of anything right now, knowing better, creature to creature. Acceptance of the spoils. A gift. A sad celebration that no one would speak into. Vacancy's momentary truce.

Cuz doused the cabin with gasoline, then scraped a match head across a torn piece of flint he fished from his pocket. Without hesitation, he threw the match into the door, feeling the heat rush out at him so that he leaned away, the short patches of hair remaining on his head feeling alive and damp. He did not fear the fire, but called to it instead, asking questions in an off-hand way. Listening, he then said, "Go a'ed 'av it. No sus fuh'kin t'ing as excident." He sensed a corner of the skin on his face cracking away in the heat, and took the thin edge between his two fingers, pulling mindfully, hoping to snag a big piece, but the skin broke away and he was noticeably disappointed by the outcome, his fingers slipping over a smooth patch of hard pink skin. He called to the dog, not waiting to watch the cabin burn. No more to say than what that violent rush of heat was making plain. Everything said, nothing explained in the grunts of human defeat. The cabin was useless to him now; his wife's presence branded along every square inch. Her smell, her laugh, and her eyes in the dark, blinking white with thoughts that he could never understand. All over it. All over him. The wholeness of the place was just as much a part of her as what they would be putting in the ground. *Ashes*, he thought. *Steam rise'n frum 'er.* He wished he could smell the final scent. His cheek pressed against her naked belly, holding her hips, holding the easy shapeliness of her hips. Fingers forgetting. *Ashes.*

Moving into the darkening woods, Cuz could not help but imagine what the man in the hospital room was guilty of; how many bodies had he uncovered and touched? Bodies that did not belong to him. And why hadn't someone already stopped him from laying his fingers where he had no right? Touching all this flesh that was now beneath his hands; the man with the long white coat and glasses to help him see plainly in such wicked brightness. No such thing as one little squint out of him. All the bodies that had been mothers and fathers, daughters and sons. Naked and touched. Cuz's wife now. The man holding firmly onto flesh and cutting, alone in the room that seemed so alive with the buzz of confusion scrubbed clean.

The ax had been sharpened only two weeks prior, and so Cuz had no trouble chipping away at the spruce boughs and placing them atop each other to form a lean-to. He did not feel like eating, and so he built no fire, despite the fact that the summer heat was cooling off, pulling back to unpin the cool forest darkness that slowly rose and lingered. The walk through the black woods had made him tired, and so he turned from where he was sitting staring into the featureless trees as if expecting to see the movements of what he was thinking, and crawled under the shield of boughs where he lay down on his sleeping bag. Sag followed in through the hole, her movements sounding loud and clear as she lumbered close to drop beside Cuz. Shifting several times. She blew out air and pressed nearer.

Wading through shallow sleep, Cuz saw a vision of the man in the dead room. He saw the man glance around the room before clicking off the lights. Silently the man left the hospital and bent into his car, staring straight through the windshield, ahead. When the engine turned over, a raccoon's tail hanging from the rearview shivered slightly, and Cuz was vaguely aware of the fact, then mildly startled by the certainty that the raccoon from the shack was missing its tail, a detail from actual life that had reinvented itself in his dream. The idea troubled him and he rolled over, grumbling, and was concerned—though not yet awake—by the presence of open space beside him. Something had been there on the ground. In his dream, he saw the man turning the ignition again, needing to provoke the engine more than once, and as the engine made its catching rumble, he saw his wife's eyes opening as if she was still dead and it was only the man with his fetish for biological mechanics that had triggered the sudden rise of her eyelids. She was lying across the back seat, one hand set against the naked coldness between her opened legs. Bolting up, she laughed and touched her chest with both her palms, before presenting the man with one of her breasts, jiggling in her cupped hands. "Yours," she said sweetly. "Take it home. Yours." What was missing? Cuz wondered. Something had been there on the ground beside him. He woke up and was alone, knowing only the stinging taste of fright in his mouth and the brutal closeness of all he had been dreaming, hating the raccoon, knowing now that it was his enemy because his dream had willfully spliced the connection.

Sag had left her place beside Cuz. Was that it; what was missing now? Cuz listened in the darkness that seeped well beyond his startled eyes to hear the vague stirrings of the dog, her paws moving quickly against the forest ground, but in the same location, as if someone was exciting her, perhaps scratching her head. He heard a voice whispering low. It was a sweet sound coming to him through the trees, through the soft yet brittle wall of boughs that surrounded him, and he realized painfully that the low pleasant sound must be the voice of a woman.

There was no moon in the sky when Cuz ducked out and straightened, keenly aware of the dark moist scent of the night earth. The movement he saw in the wall of black trees could have been anything. The movement was ten times blacker than he thought himself capable of sighting, the denseness full-bodied and leaking away from itself, and a voice seemed not to be moving with this mass that shifted in the trees. The restless voice sang low and sugary, without words, only breathy sounds, all around him, and the bulk of something that moved apprehensively, as if on its own, but trying to find the voice that surely belonged to it. Sag was there with her legs stumbling. Cuz could hear the paw-moving sounds of the dog, and her short bursts of whining, following the movement of whatever it was, but her dog ears confused by the voice that was coming from everywhere at once.

A lovely scent visited Cuz, a whiff of roses and lemons pleasing him, and he realized that he would be seeing someone soon, someone he did not expect, reaching forward from the trees, a woman's stiff arm coming white through the branches, but he was wrong. There was no arm. The first thing that came was the pale slant of a naked leg, stepping forward, then the lower body and the black-red shading of glistening pubic hair, alive and stirring, fibers bending to blindly feel the skin they were fastened to. And then the second leg revealed beneath the spill of moonlight that bravely freed itself from behind a gray cloud. A corner of the moon uncovered and uncovering a section of the body, before the woman stepped freely from the trees and stood watching him, with Sag's wrinkled face looking up at Cuz, then at the woman, as if wanting to prompt acknowledgement.

The woman smiled, her hands beside her square naked hips, her breasts full, their black-red nipples studded with seeds, like ripe berries about to drop from the veinwork of branches that stretched inside of her, needing to find root elsewhere. The nipples falling off, seed by seed, with new ones pushing out. Bending slowly at the knees, the woman patted the dog. Cuz watched without comment, held only by the love that settled through every inch of him. He felt that he should speak and so he said, "Do ya wan' sum clo's?" The pleasant woman shook her head without a word, then opened her lips, but waited before she said, "What for? I'm not cold." Standing and stepping closer, the woman appeared familiar. She was not his wife, but Cuz thought there was a slight resemblance, and he wondered what she was doing here, lost in the woods.

"I should be the one asking you; what're you doing lost in the woods?"

Cuz had not said a word, and he wondered how the woman

had known. Feeling frightened and angry, he retorted, "I'm naw laws'd."

"Come here," said the woman, and Cuz went closer until the woman kissed him and a rush of color that was the color of his dead wife raced through her skin.

"Ooow," the woman thrilled, with her eyes closed. She jerked her neck and carefully shook her wrists, as if trying to loosen something. Soon the color of his dead wife left the woman and she was perfectly white again, as if her skin was thick and polished and beautifully clean.

The woman opened her eyes. "I can't touch you now, Cuz," she told him.

Cuz said his wife's name, but the woman did not seem to notice what he was saying. A moment later she shook her head. "I'm sorry you don't understand." Her smile so soft and becoming. "It's impossible to explain."

Cuz thought that she was someone very different, someone wild but holding back, tamed in a way that made her happy, and Sag stayed close to the woman's legs, knowing by the scent that she was who she was, no matter how she happened to appear.

"Do you want me?" the woman asked. Without answering, Cuz turned away and dropped to his knees, crawling into the lean-to. He lay down and shut his eyes, repeating the crying word "help" inside his head, but it was not so loud, more like a prayer than a shout. He told himself to go to sleep, but he was cold. When he opened his eyes again, the woman was lying beside him, her green and brown and blue eyes watching him up close, her body white and smelling warm and powdery. She kissed his cheek and half of her face flushed green. She rubbed it with her fingers, grimacing slightly, but in a way that made Cuz think of pleasure.

"Wha're ya affer, womb'n?"

"Cuz." The woman smiled and reached between her legs, yanking out a silent white baby and tossing it toward the low roof of the lean-to where it hovered weightlessly, glancing down and fluttering its tiny fingers close to its face, before giggling and slowly drifting through the boughs.

"Don't touch me," the woman whispered, shutting her eyes cozily. "Just don't. Passion works instantly now. The mere thought of such emotions inspires immediate conception. The way it was meant to be."

Cuz understood that the woman was strangely mad, like the village idiots he remembered seeing throughout the years in Cutland Junction. Love melding with fear, he rolled away from her, over on his side, but felt her warm breath against his neck, prompting him to roll back again, to view her face gone green, her eyes larger and her lips coming forward, soon on him, and they were blue like in the winter when the body stays out too long against the elements that mean to take something from you, something that belongs back with the woods and the water and air, a scrap of vastness that was once part of a whole but now wrongly set in one broken, misdirected person.

"On top of me," she said. "Do what you intended, what you thought would bring me back." Clutching him with her hands, she easily lifted him on top of her and reached down to take hold of his prick, to force entry. Cuz felt himself growing into her, as if reaching into warm mud that was cooling. And he knew that he must love her so fiercely that she would die, kill her with the scalding semen that was sure to erase her, or do something much different from killing, something well beyond killing, for which there was no given name, for she was already dead. But the idea of killing was close enough. It would lead him toward whatever it was that he was really trying to do. The woman closed her thighs on him so that he could not pull himself free from where he was lodged inside her.

"Let it loose," she said. "Please, sweetheart." Her lips splitting and hardening. She could barely speak, her eyelids cracking, like the burnt skin across Cuz's face, small flakes falling against her yellowing eyeballs. They were both coming apart, and it was all by accident.

Cuz thought of the occurrences that had named themselves accidents—the unbalancing of objects wiping things out and replacing them with holes that were to be filled painfully by acceptance of the sorrow, or the repositioning of other, newer bodies into the places of those lost. Thinking such bold, frightening thoughts, Cuz could not hold back any longer. He tried to draw away, tightening the muscles around his groin, shrinking back into himself, not wanting to make her pregnant, but really needing to more than anything. Punching free, the ejaculation tore something from him, an urge or an understanding not yet complete, and the woman smiled, saying, "Now, what does that prove?" before turning to dust beneath him. Unsupported, his body thudded to the ground, his face against the musky grass. When he rolled to his side and turned his head toward the opening of the lean-to, he saw Sag standing there in the narrow hole with her face hanging loose and horribly sad. A form was standing on the dog's back, and Cuz saw that it was the raccoon, its tiny paws in front of its face, sloppily rubbing against each other, as if clapping at the farcical outcome of what it had just been fortunate enough to witness.

Cuz took it as a dream. Although waking in the morning, he was uncertain if the dream still held him. With a lingering sense of detachment, he packed up his duffel bag and wandered off. The sunlight through the green and gray branches was reassuring and he could see everything. In this broad clarity, there was no question whatsoever about things moving around without being identified for what they truly were.

Walking all day, deeper and deeper into the woods, through brief clearings and back into the shadowed denseness of trees that tried to hold him, he trudged until dusk pulled those shadows from the woods across a new, bigger clearing where he stopped, sighting a lake where Sag was bent to take a drink. Cuz decided that this would be a good place to camp for the night. The gentle lapping of the water was calming, reassuring. He was a man again, in the woods with his dog. It was as simple as that. A male body. Solid with the land. No dreams needed here.

Done with her sloppy drinking, Sag wandered off, lifting her head and staring into the trees, then sniffing the cool grass, lifting her gaze and shaking her head, her ears flapping back and forth, her nose soon low to the earth again, the skin along her mouth jiggling as she worked her way toward a bark.

Cuz took his ax from his duffel bag and purposefully strolled across the green and yellow grass to the edge of the treeline, where he cut several boughs. When he returned to collect his duffel bag and call for Sag, he noticed how the light had retracted farther into the trees, the shadows so long they were almost spread along the entire stretch of space before and around him, but he could still stand in the narrow orange slants of light set between the shadows, the remaining tempered heat richly spilling across his face.

"Ey?" he called to Sag. Listening, he heard a crow cawing and the swooping flight of a bird overhead, before realizing the frantic sounds of paws racing through the woods, then the howling that Cuz had not heard in quite a while. It was a call of pursuit. He followed the sound. Eyes skimming the treeline, he saw Sag breaking through the tangled edge, flushing the creature that waddled quickly ahead, running to the edge of the lake and racing in. Sag strode close behind, making a lot of noise as she splashed toward the deeper water, then swam smoothly, but desperately, after the escaping raccoon.

Once closer to the water, Cuz saw by the wake of where it was swimming that the raccoon's tail was missing. It swam, as if with certain purpose, but lack of concern, toward the middle of the lake, before pausing, turning to face the bloodhound, waiting for the dog to find its way closer, waiting with a single idea suspending it in the water. Sag struggled to reach the center; she was old and determined and paddled with great effort toward the raccoon. Cuz smiled at the sight of Sag and the game she was playing, but he wondered why the raccoon had stopped now and was waiting in an almost friendly way as Sag labored nearer, directly toward the raccoon that easily circled behind the dog and climbed onto her back. Expecting to see the raccoon brush its paws together as in his dream, Cuz stared with numb interest, sensing the tingling fear rise in his mouth again, the matching of disaster with the brewing of sleepy suspicions. He drifted closer to the edge of the lake, seeing so clearly he was rendered immobile for an instant. A breath, then one insensible step into the shallowest part of the water.

The raccoon took its time wobbling up the length of the bloodhound's back as Sag turned in slow circles before frantically deciding to paddle clumsily toward the shore. The raccoon continued its slow jolly walk until it paused, resting on the top of Sag's head, the weight pressing the dog's muzzle beneath the surface of the water. The raccoon remained in place until all movements ceased from the dog, then it slid into the water and swam effortlessly in the other direction, toward the farthest shore.

Cuz stood in disbelief, witnessing the heavy body of the dog slowly rolling over in the water. He realized that it was not a replay of a dream at all. It was something he had not expected, something he could not have anticipated. All of it was real and seemed physically attached to him, more frighteningly clear than any dream could possibly be.

The following day, Cuz returned to the police station in Cutland Junction, confessing to the policeman that he had killed his wife two nights ago in the woods.

"I kill'd 'er 'cause I cud'nt bare ta see 'er da way she was so perfuk. It 'armed me eyes. It made me stumuk vomit. She turn ta dust. Was 'er all over a'gin. I try ta bring 'er back, but all I's did was kill 'er and kill 'er more."

The policeman took Cuz to the dead room and again showed him the body of his wife that had been held for pickup. The body was white and drained and pure. A thick Y-shaped scar ran from her shoulders down across her breasts, connecting at the top of her belly before continuing down to the space between her legs. The ridges of the scar were neat and perfectly white with no pinkness. The pinkness now gone. She was changed again, put back together, and Cuz agreed that the woman he had killed did not look much like his wife, but he knew that it was his wife all the same. The woman had crumbled right out from under him, turned to dust in the blink of an eye, he told the two men.

"It's okay," said the policeman.

"We need to bury her soon," the man with the glasses calmly declared, pulling the sheet back up. "We never hold bodies here for long. But I was . . ." He stretched his lips with a quiet, even gesture of resignation, ". . . waiting." And he nodded with relief as he straightened his glasses with two fingers.

"She aw'rady gone," Cuz said to them both. His left eye was almost swollen shut from the smooth fire scars on his face, but he could still blink away the tears. The two men looked at him, understanding the need to hold their expressions as plain as possible.

"Let's go," the policeman said. "It was an accident, Cuz. You didn't do anything."

"I di'nt," Cuz blurted out. "I dee'd."

"Come on outside," said the policeman, gently laying his hand against Cuz's solid back.

The man in the room watched the door swing closed as the two men slowly moved out. He waited for silence, stillness before telling himself that he had never seen such a display before. The woman's husband, the man named Cuz, had such a ghoulish face. It was frightening the way he looked and the way he talked, too, particularly when he cried. It was an absolutely terrifying sight. The man in the room shuddered, glad that Cuz was no longer present. He breathed a slow sigh of relief, using both hands to carefully push shut the shiny heavy drawer where the woman's body lay. Snapping off his plastic gloves, he stepped across the room, struck by a troubling sight as he observed the row of specimen jars along the cool silver ledge. Something was definitely wrong here. He stared beyond the glass into its contents that rested there so obligingly. He wondered until he was almost worried, then realized he was looking much too closely. What a gift to possess the good grace that afforded one the most reasonable of conclusions. He smiled to himself and took one step back, focusing on the exact surfaces and edges. He saw what was important now. Of course, the line of jars was merely out of order, crooked, simply in need of straightening.

The Story of an Eye
by Norman Ravvin

I've been told that in the old country they brought a sick man a pineapple, the sort of fruit that was nearly impossible to find, so its arrival would strike him as a magical act, a bright omen. Nobody gave me a pineapple. In fact, once I'd started home, just barely staying on my feet, a kid coming out of a greasy spoon yelled something and elbowed me out of his way. That was on Drake. I landed on the grass by the roadside and someone lifted my foot off the pavement so it wouldn't be run over. I heard a voice ask, "Are you okay?" But whoever it was had gone before I could answer.

What followed is mostly a blur to me, and I can remember only bits and pieces. The clouds making way for the moon and glowing silver over the mountains. The swirl of fruit flies over the doorstep of the building on Georgia Street. In the alleys, ragged men digging in dumpsters for half-eaten food. When I saw the sign above a door on Homer that read "Wood Laboratory, Chemists, Bacteriologists," I realized I was heading in the wrong direction, and I turned myself around and walked west over the bridge toward where I live. I felt like a cartoon character, crawling in the desert with his clothes in rags, keeping an eye out for a mirage of kindness.

I used to tell my students—it drove them crazy with boredom—that in the old country you couldn't get a nectarine or a pineapple. Here you can get anything you like. Poor men grow up to run empires. Every day I see people in my neighborhood who look like gods—men with their chests bursting, women with their heels dug deep in the earth. I can sense their pleasure, their satisfaction; it trails behind them like musk. They don't have any trouble looking beautiful as long as they're safe among their treasure. It's when you're solitary, scattered, struggling under the gaze of strangers, that you start to feel ugly and tired. And I do. I'll be the first to admit it.

It's been a year since I worked, and a couple of months since I talked to anyone other than the mailman or the check-out clerk at the corner store. I've let myself go. I've let things happen that I never thought would happen to me, only to others. I've begun to look like a bum. That's a word you used to hear a lot. What do social workers say nowadays? Person of the Street? That sounds almost alluring—an exotic career—like Lady of the Night. But there are variations on the theme I haven't tried yet. I don't drink aftershave on park benches. I'm no junkie, no beggar, no digger in dumpsters. I still know the year and the day and my name, and I can recognize the way others look at me; but still, I've begun to look like a bum. I have an unacceptable scent. It's not that I smell of sweat or urine or of airless rooms. I smell organic, alive. But not human. Humans smell of soap, spice, pressed cotton. Those are human smells, though it's a funny thing to consider.

Where I grew up, apples dropped in the grass in the dark. Autumn light fell in yellow bands through the picket fence. There was a deep closet full of clean linen, fresh towels, furled umbrellas. I'll take you there some time. If we cross town, turn left, open the gate and ring the bell, I'm sure someone will be home to show us what's in that closet.

I've almost forgotten what it was like to work. To get up each morning and have somewhere familiar to go. I enjoyed my job, the kids, the school. I always thought of myself as a good teacher. And now I don't remember how it all came unraveled. Something to do with hands and hair. I couldn't make sense of it at the time, and I'm not much clearer about it now. But summer came, and I was cleaning out my office instead of looking forward to the fall.

I still thought for a time I would get back to it, back to work. But a year has passed; I've got what's left of my severance to pay the rent, and I'm bursting with boredom and bad premonitions. I'm not fit to be a teacher anymore.

I was ashamed of myself this morning when the young man saw me coming up the street. He was surprised at first, but then he looked worried. I walked toward him, naked below my shirt, an awful dark mess where my left eye should have been. All the way home from downtown, across the bridge and through the quiet neighborhoods, I'd been telling myself it was just swollen shut, badly bruised, that it would surely heal and open again. But the way he looked at me erased any hope I'd had.

He told me to stay put, and he ran back to the place where he worked. I suppose he was looking for a towel or a blanket, but all he came up with was a mail bag. A canvas Canada Post mail bag. I held it around myself like a skirt, but it kept falling, and he helped me readjust it, though I could tell he didn't really like the idea of touching me. I was a strange, incomprehensible obscenity: a half-naked, newly made invalid trying to get home.

That was his first suggestion. He'd take me home. But somehow the directions I gave him and the way he heard them didn't jibe. I knew, in the dark, behind my closed eye, that we were less than a block away from my apartment. But we managed to walk up the street and back, the mail bag slipping and passers-by looking at us as if we were ghosts, before he got me back to the building where I live.

And, of course, I'd lost the key to the front door. I told my guide he could leave, that I would just wait for the first tenant to come by who would let me inside. But he had no intention of doing that. He insisted on calling an ambulance, because he thought, if I didn't attend to what remained of the left eye, the right one would be lost, too. I honestly didn't care. I'd have given them both to have the whole thing over. I knew that with an ambulance comes a police car, that the police ask for next of kin and I have none, and that my landlord had been searching high and low for a reason to evict me. The obvious solution would be to drop me off at the mental health center. That's what the cops are trained to do with difficult cases. They drop them off and let things work themselves out.

At the school where I taught, it was hands and hair. But I wasn't trying to accost anyone, or take advantage of their innocence, as the complaint against me implied. There's no pleasure in taking advantage, just as there is none in being taken advantage of. But there didn't seem to be a way of countering my colleagues' arguments against me: my teaching reports were excellent, but they had become convinced that they wanted me gone, because of who I am.

For some time I've been visiting the paths that cross the center of Stanley Park where men go to meet. There's busy traffic there after work hours, boys and grandfathers, office workers in short-sleeve shirts. But hidden among this crowd is the odd fearful outsider, a kind of hunter. And my judgement is so bad. I always pick the ones who've come out of fear. The ones who've made an agreement with themselves about who it is they hate, who it is they would rather see dead than alive. My choosing these types must say something about me, but I don't care to look into it very deeply. It's much too late for that.

The reason I know better than to trust the police, or the ambulance men for that matter, is because I know they have the same cold thoughts as the men in the park who've made up their minds. And when I look at it that way, I realize I'm no safer in the hands of the authorities than I was in the shadows, among the cedar and the stinkweed below Lumberman's Arch. That's where it began. I could see the pyramids of sulfur and flat-topped hills of sawdust across the inlet; I could see a flash of red azaleas against the violet water; I could see the bulk of the bridge's span disappearing behind a bend, and fallen trees draped in dirty cobwebs. The obligatory "Jesus Saves" was sprayed on a pedestrian overpass in orange neon paint. As if in answer to this, someone had etched "BRIDGE OF DEATH" in black on a pylon seeping mossy water. The past fall's leaves gathered around me in gullies like the beds of fallen angels. And the air was cool as I walked through the dankness until I came upon Beaver Lake, which is surrounded by a climate from another hemisphere. Coming upon it is like stepping out of one world and into another. The stalled water and the protective walls of the surrounding forest gather the summer heat and hold it.

I saw, sitting in the shade, in the cool of a forgotten season, two men. They seemed to beckon to me from across the lake so I walked toward them. As I went I felt the afternoon slowing down, heating up, and everything around took on the strangest clarity. Lily pads—half green, half burgundy—shifted on the lake. Ducks flashed their green foreheads at me, their orange sideburns. Steam rose off the wet logs gathered at the water's edge; and along the shallow corners of the lake, pike sculled on the muddy bottom.

As I came close, the two men rose from the bench where they sat and disappeared into the forest. I followed, watching as they stopped in a clearing. Light streamed around them—over their shoulders and between their legs.

But, of course, it was all a mistake. A misunderstanding. By the time they had finished with me, it was getting dark, and I saw my blood in dark patches on the dirt. I lay there, trying to coax myself up, but the feeling in my belly was terrible, and the left eye—the dark one—gave the impression that the top half of the world had disappeared. As I lay, listening, I became aware that at twilight objects often start to make odd sounds and fall apart.

It took me all night to find my way home. And by the time I arrived back at the street where I live, to the horror of the man who offered me the mail bag, I must have looked like spent fruit, the flesh of the inside of my cheek showing and the left eye gone. Naked below my shirt, hands hanging in a pathetic effort at modesty, I heard myself say, "I don't want to be a bother. I'll find my way..."

By the time the ambulance arrived, one of the tenants from

my building was telling my helper, loudly, as if I were deaf or not there, that they'd been trying to evict me, that they'd had to renovate the house around me, that the smells from my apartment seeped like poisonous gas into the neighboring rooms. "It's worse than Chernobyl," I heard the young woman yell, as the tanned ambulance attendant fixed me tightly to the stretcher. His face was blank. Uninterested in my condition, he was thinking of his girlfriend, of donuts, of the weather.

When I looked up at the man who'd brought me the mail bag, I could see that he hated himself for having called the authorities, though all he'd meant to do was save my one good eye. I think he knew then that I'd have given my right eye simply to get inside, go upstairs, and lie down in the dark. In his way, though, he'd meant well, and I regretted, as I was lifted into the back of the van, that we'd not met under better circumstances. As the back gate of the van slammed shut, I heard pineapples plummeting to earth, nectarines falling softly in the dark.

These Are Ghost Stories
by Elyse Gasco

He who cannot howl
Will not find his pack...
—Charles Simic

These are ghost stories hunters tell of the ones that got away. Not the ones that almost got away, that seemed only to blend momentarily with whatever they were hiding behind, the browns and yellows of hunting season. Nor the ones they did get with crisp, clean shots that made these hunters drop their guns with a yelp and dance a weird, manly minuet. Choked with joy they slap each other's strong backs; but these are not the stories that haunt them. The heads they hang above their fireplaces, quietly stunned, professionally stuffed, lovingly preserved, these are just whores to them, easy prey that seemed almost to mount themselves willingly on the den walls. No, they tell stories only of the ones that stared them down and outran their bullets and seemed to disappear magically into the woods; or the ones that made mud and shrubs, fallen trees and sudden storms appear from nowhere; or the ones that in freak confrontations and terrible bellowing escaped with the rifles hitched to their antlers. These are the ones that keep them up at night, thinking they hear animal grunting somewhere, respectfully loathing the ones who would not be cowed.

* * *

Realize that these are days of strange imaginings. The eyes of people you know; the eyes of strangers are flat as the side of an eel. Those with myopia are letting their glasses hang from their necks on string, preferring the soft edges of blurred objects. No one can decide if the affliction is insomnia, or just too much sleep. Faces seem creased, like tangled bed sheets. The sky of night and day seems just the same: a soft gray—the night not quite dark enough, the yellow of the day somehow gagged. Someone in power is putting up signs that say: Just keep busy.

In a dream, great bombs explode a zoo. Iron bars are blown from cages, and the rubble makes bridges across the moats of the big animals. Lions meet up with hyenas again; eland and musk oxen, oryx and ibex nod their heavy heads to each other in greeting and, free, they run straight towards the fire.

The Head is disenchanted with the world. Cameras catch him sleeping, the sensitive microphones pick up the guttural snores and the labored breathing. Sometimes he appears just as a yawn, the wide opening of his mouth, the silver of his fillings, the strands of saliva, his sour breath fogging up the cameras when they get too close. I guess I am just bored, says the Head to his people. Complete ennui, he says, smiling at his awful accent. The Head is usually shy and sleepy, and so everyone is surprised when he calls the press to gather round and listen well. He yawns and says: I am too tired to name this war. And so he announces a contest and suggestions are to be mailed in to a certain media station, or dropped into a metal box at the local supermarket. The Head wonders about the theme music. The only thing he knows for sure is that there should be oboes, but no flutes.

* * *

Mark this. It is the year your magical birth mother, the one you hunted down and captured in an impressive display of prowess (okay, maybe it wasn't really prowess, maybe you only came upon her like a dog catcher), declares that she has nothing left to say and stops talking. It is also the year that too many people are having near-death experiences without ever actually dying, without actually experiencing any real bodily harm, no straining or bursting organs, no blood or draining fluids, not even rotting gums or paper cuts. Just people who suddenly and absolutely in the middle of their lives unfasten themselves from their ordinary moments and launch their tiny spirits like shuttles high above themselves. It is as though everyone is filled with a great wanting, a hunger to float high above their bodies and look down on the world with a cool and lofty detachment, that someone says is like being the moon.

A woman wades through the water, her ankles and shins slick with black oil; around her sea birds, their greasy feathers plastered to their bodies, stiff like little soldiers. She describes lifting off out of her body—not exactly flying; more like rising (bubbles to the top of the glass)—and a clear white light and smooth friendly hands that reach to her in love. A child, a television, a gun, and a bad joke on every station; a woman sells him a car in her underwear, and suddenly he is moving like a ghost train through a tunnel and all around him he hears voices saying: We love you. A man steps over a body in the street and describes a rush of clean wind, a light that called itself love and a sudden soaring sense of peace that fills him up like medicine in a syringe.

Some blame it on the gaping ozone layer. Still others insist that finally the opaque film between the living and the dead is dissolving, running down like cheap watercolors, leaving clear white spaces. There is even talk of evolution and metamorphosis, likening it to the great slimy hoist from sea to land. But everyone who has been there is eerily unafraid of death; the suicide hotlines are jammed, and no one is wearing a seat belt.

It is also the year you abandon your impossible collages—wood on paper, lead on silk; things that pull everything out of shape and hang mean and heavy, like teeth from a thread of skin, it makes your gums ache just to look at them—and begin carving tools and amulets for the new millennium, believing that there must be something you can make with your hands that might stop the world.

* * *

I love you, says the Head one night in your living room, terrifically awake for a few brief seconds, throwing out his arms to the world. I love you, he says again. And don't you always hurt the ones you love? This is a rhetorical question and not a contest, and so no one is expected to mail in a response.

* * *

The first thing you do is forbid the word "love" in your home. Because lately, when you look at your man, all you feel like doing is hunting, and except accidentally, you've never killed anything before in your life. Maybe it is because he is already wounded that you pick him out from the rest. Maybe it is because you can smell the rawness in his flesh. But lately, when you look at him, you sing an improvised song, a melody that might lull him to take a few steps closer even though he can smell the danger everywhere, a song that shifts the wind just the right way so that you can ask him—deer, hog, wild-animal husband—if on this day he would be willing to die for you. You know that he must be a willing victim, that this is a conversation of death; eye to eye you each admit that it is time, and that if the hunt does not go well, he might haunt you forever with his unhappiness. And when you eat of his flesh you will assume his power; but this you recognize is not love. You forbid the word "love" in your small world because really, what do you know of it anyway? Your heart, too busy with its own self-absorbed, monotonous lub-dub to pay much attention to anything else; trapped in its little rib cage, like a zoo animal, or behind the bars of a crib, like an infant, suckling and unforgiving—give me, give me. And you realize that sometimes a kiss is not a kiss, but just a way of stopping his mouth.

* * *

The Head says that if there is fighting it will be done shoeless, maybe even naked. He flirts with the warriors, who eagerly strip for him and fall over from exhausted love, their bloody lips puckered to the ground. He bats his sleepy eyelashes and runs a perfumed wrist across their throats, down their knobby spines. He mesmerizes them with his flashy teeth and callused palms. They would throw their full jackets over puddles for him; they would pick him up and carry his body over oceans; all he has to do is mention love, and they are his. If only he was not so fickle and bored. If only he did not fall asleep so quickly. This army fatigues. This land forces them to stay hard. They practice marching barefoot. The earth is softer than they imagined. They kick at it to see if there is still life there, the way you roll a dead thing over, kicking at the belly, the inside of a thigh, just to make sure it isn't faking. But to toughen up their soles, the Head forces them to dance for him on thistle and stones, rocks and thorns, and so they pound the earth.

* * *

You knew when you brought him home that he was not a poet, though his condensed language and short sentences fooled you at first, and if sometimes he couldn't finish a thought or even an emotion, well, maybe that was like not going all the way to the end of the page, a whole empty white margin just waiting there on the right side. Still, you are never quite ready for this quick change in rhythm, when the unstressed suddenly becomes stressed, when the heart does an unexpected dip that almost makes you lose your balance, that almost stops you dead. The truth is that sometimes when he smiles at you, you can see past the teeth and gums and jaw to the kind of skull he will be in the ground, and when he holds your hand, you watch his fingers close around your wrist and are surprised to see how little skin you both have, as though your skeletons were floating to the top of your body, bobbing there just below the surface. And in bed your bones clank together like dishes. You begin to call it "The Death of the Passion," and you think there should be some ceremony for it: a ritual, a kind of frenzied dancing to celebrate this bloodless passing. So you are surprised to find this note in the center of your white pillow, pinned there like a voodoo doll:

> *Shatter my heart*
> *So a new room can be created*
> *For a limitless love*
>   *—A Sufi Prayer*

You turn to him lying there beside you, straight as a wooden spear, but he is already asleep and the wind blows through him, whistling.

* * *

To stand near death and not go floating out of your body, this to you seems like a real challenge. You know that there are people who enter their great family tombs to dust the bones of loved ones and murmur news and gossip to the powdered past. Here the living whisper love to the dead, and no ghostly hookers stand at the doorway reaching out with perfumed hands for anything they can grab. Things are always dying and yet you can find so few remains. Where are all the skulls and bones? You are sure that things must have died in your backyard, but you cannot find any evidence. Even the dogs are digging and coming up with nothing. Archeologists have found bones with notches carved in them, bone slates inscribed as markers or reminders: maybe the lunar cycle, or perhaps a great ceremony or an anticipated voyage. It is not this primitive Filofax system that interests you so much, but that they walked around with bones in their pockets and pouches, so near death but with two dirty, hairy feet firmly rooted in the earth.

This is all that you are thinking as you watch him curl into bed naked, bent down on his hands and knees scraping the dog hair from the mattress and scattering it to the floor in little gray balls; magical hair that can keep growing for a little while even after death. These are your nighttime rituals: the hair and skin falling to the ground which you will sweep away in the morning, and the calling of the dogs back to the bed where one settles in his arms around him and the other brings her rawhide to you and settles across your legs to gnaw until she grows sleepy. These are bedtime ghost stories, this assembling and rearranging of bones, each shifting position, each movement, each turning, like different vignettes telling the story of night and morning. He turns to you tonight, and though you are aching for it to feel like ritual, frightening and mysterious, something done in a mask to the sound of drum beats, it feels only like a dark black habit, something a nun might wear. You know that sometimes by repetition there is magic, but tonight it feels only like two sticks rubbing against each other hoping for fire and instead only scraping your skin down to a dangerous point. You imagine him rising up and slipping out of himself, his deceitful spirit as oily and spongy as moss.

Someone blinds him with a white light and declares her awful love, and he doesn't want to come back. So you say to him—just for an edge of drama, just to give him something to think about:

Sometimes I look at you and I can almost see what you'll look like decomposing. And this makes you think of your daughter who one day for your pleasure defined decomposing as Mozart in the ground with no songs left to write. You let him wipe you like a baby while you lie back and watch his pointy face, his jutting jaw lit up by the blue light of darkness. He says: You must stop imagining that this is the end of the world. You know that he is speaking relatively, but you also know, just the way Einstein knew, that imagination is more important than knowledge.

* * *

The day your mother stopped talking, she said that she believed that she never really had anything to teach you, and so what was the point of going on, babbling, chitchatting; what were you really saying to each other anyway? Everything would simply be repetition and polite, but meaningless, conversation of things you already knew and that would only make you both sad and edgy. Some relationships are just filled with regret from the start. All that is possible, she said, all that has ever been possible between us, between everybody, is complete misunderstanding. Let's not embarrass ourselves. Let's just be very, very quiet. Think of it as an oath. This is the last thing she ever said to you, her voice gray and monotone as though she was trying to drive you away with her dullness. What does this word mean? your daughter used to ask, pointing at anything: the rows of spice jars, a newspaper headline, your doodles beside the telephone, the labels of her clothing. And you would think, how deep to ask the meanings when all you could ever give her were the sketchy boundaries of a word, and finally her turning to you and saying, It doesn't mean anything unless you think it does, does it? And that night she stopped sleeping in your bed, her warm wiggling body trying so hard to be still. In the end, you want to believe in the solemnity of your mother's vow, that maybe it is possible to make words sacred again, to start over by not speaking. She sends you only one letter and it says: Don't be sad. I looked it up in the dictionary: "Mum" means silent, say nothing.

It seems everyone around you is growing weary and quiet. Lately it seems to you that even your man has run out of questions, as though he imagined that you were something already answered, an equation old and solved, as though after he asked you to marry him he ran out of questions, or maybe the ceremony made him think that two-word answers would always do. But like a weary troubadour he keeps reciting his lines by heart—how are you what did you do today good-night, and all that—but you wonder every minute where his mind is, what he thinks of when he looks at you, why he is no longer curious, and you worry all the time that he is just about to leave his body. You imagine he will be blameless, that he will say to you: I didn't fall out of love. I was pushed.

But no. This is not quite right. You have never really wanted his questions, have always been terrible at answering his questions, probing him for his most secret fantasies, his most embarrassing moments, his deepest hurts, and he gushed like a vein, and really, didn't you just lick up the blood or enact his desires, anything to keep from having to answer any of these things about yourself. What you always wanted were his proclamations, to be emblazoned by his voice, sung into existence like some tribal custom that sings the sun back into the sky, the rocks back into formation, for him to know you or even pretend to know you without your having to say a word. You have always wanted to be somebody's song, some woman who he thinks talks to angels, who can call the stars down to her feet, who could walk with animals and tame everything she sees. Even if it was all wrong, even if it was all a lie, just to watch him trying to put you together in magical notes, something he could hum all day long. Don't you ever think of me during the day? you used to ask him. But he could only take the question apart, never put it back together. What did you mean by "think"? What did you mean by "you"? Sometimes he would see your anguish and say: Well, give me the lines, tell me what to say, start me off. As though you really were a song, but one that he'd forgotten, one that if you hummed a few bars it just might come back to him. But feeding him his lines, string by string like worms, strumming the chord to start him off or to clear his throat by, made it seem cheap, bird-like: Just open your ugly blue throat and I will feed you myself. You have always wanted him to be, to be, to be an empath your daughter says, and you wonder how she knew what you were thinking. Yes, an empath or a prophet, at the very least a Fury, something that wanted to follow you around, that had the stamina to haunt you. But you can even become bored of a haunting. Surely, you must get tired of your ghosts and devils. Oh, the toilet is just overflowing blood and slime again. And there goes that black gunk down the wall again. Sometimes, the minute you say, I know, you stop listening. You put a little cage around your bird man, and he puts another around you, and all the shuffling and movement is just swinging on the fake wood perch, whistling at each other through the bars. Sometimes when you watch him sleep you get a glimpse of how infinite he might be, and you remember a time when sleep was only necessary and not a way of flight, and you remember waking him up with your mouth, and how he called it deadly soft, and now you think to yourself: All the better to succubi.

* * *

It is amazing the people you let into your home. The anchor man throws out his heavy steel hook and then he is moored there, his great ship nearly taking over your living room. His face presses up against the glass porthole; his tie hangs flaccid. He reads a list of possible war names: The New Clear Vision, Atom and Grieve,

The Real Thing. Children are fond of The Big Mac Attack: the hamburger meat of war, all of life melting like cheese in its boots, over a billion sold and all that, and extra ketchup for the pretend battle. But the Head, rightly so, is unsatisfied, and so the search goes on for the absolute pun, the last perfect metaphor, the simile that will once and for all encapsulate what war is like.

* * *

For your birth mother you sew together pouches and purses to hold stones and charms and magic herbs. For her you sew up holes in stray socks, buttons onto stiff shirts, the gaping mouth of a down pillow that is spewing up feathers, suturing up anything that needs to be closed and tight. At night your man is called in on an emergency. A spayed dog has eaten through her stitches. Her people found her on their bed chewing away at her own guts, and in their panic they called to say that their dog was inside out.

And this is taped to the center of your mirror; where your eyes would meet your eyes instead you see:

My desert woman, my she-wolf, my furious wife
    I know your blood, your smell, your fire
And I follow like a hound to the borderland
    of your desire, to the very tip of your knife

* * *

The second thing you must do is pretend to die like a tree; the way they fake their sentimental, technicolor autumn passing, and hang around, a forest of twigs and wooden crosses, only to taunt and dazzle with their resurrection.

Your daughter is a little witch and you are endlessly enchanted by her, though she does not know yet what she can do. You want to make all her equipment by hand, her clothing, her tools, her jewels and talismans, so that everywhere she goes she will feel your palms urging her forward, the work of your fingertips, the imprint of you, massaging her instincts back into a muscle. She is near womanhood, the hood cloaking her in a new disguise that you are not used to, or the hood that is the folds of the skin near the head of the cobra that expands before it strikes, or the hood that is your little hoodlum, a street toughy, unafraid—and now you know you cannot stop yourself, that thoughts of her send you free associating—her little red riding hood, the dark forest where she will teach herself pleasure and self-sufficiency. You know that there are tribes where a mother must prepare her daughter—not to close her up but to make her open, to tear the delicate skin, the thin membrane—with whatever: a fruit, a blessed branch, an oiled broom handle. And you imagine that it means that no man can ever plant his flag and claim discovery of that land, for surely there are natives living there. Or better still, more magically, more bizarre, more horrible, the mother breaks through her daughter and says: As you tore through me so shall I tear through you.

But here there are no initiations, no hot coals to cross, no animals to hunt, no way to prove our worthiness to ourselves, and all the scars we leave are unintentional. And all at once everyone stops talking and we must pay our shamans just to listen to us and even they are methodically silent. You spend your whole life questing after the woman you were born to, and suddenly she decides to go mute and weird, like a cult leader you just can't get close to. The artist says there are no lines, only patches of color, one beside the other, and you used to think this was true. Think of your daughter's soft translucent skin and blue blood pumping so close to the surface beside your thick veiny breasts, her puff of black smoky hair against your bronzed knees, her coral patch of lips easily whispering into your cold red ears. But now you can see the lines forming, as she delineates and you wrinkle slightly, from the smile curve of her hips to the smile curves by your eyes. It is more like an etching now, or a deep wood carving. You cut food together in the kitchen, preparing for a feast. She is deft with a knife and is in charge of the herbs. You watch her chopping mint and basil, the flash of the knife thrilling you, maybe there will be blood, maybe there will be a ceremony after all, and you can feel the expression on your face, that flat smug closed mouth smile, the love pumping out of your misty eyes, just like the soup-commercial mother, and you think: Please let me give her something better than chunks in a can. You want to give her spells, charms, fire, a howl to raise the hackles on any animal's back. She kisses your hands that are coated in garlic and sticky against her lips. She says: Mom, do you ever get that not-so-fresh feeling? She must see you getting ready to leave your body—the way your eyes are contracting as though suddenly you were blinded by a great white light, the way your skin is beginning to sag as though you were being sucked by a water bug—because she is tugging you down by the braid of your hair saying: It's a joke, Mom. A joke.

* * *

Maybe it isn't true that there aren't any rituals. Maybe it is only that like love, they are so personal, so highly individualized that they are almost psychotic. In the beginning, when the garden is lush and ripe with fruit and you still walk around naked for each other, you practice his leaving. Once, you left someone, and you thought you could keep the evil spell of repetition away by practicing hard enough so that you might bore the Fates into leaving you alone. Oh yes, you say to the mirror, the sofa, the painted armoire, I understand exactly why you have to go. You practice being calm and accepting. Once you even offer to help him pack his things, and your hands mime the precise folding of his shirts;

but this makes you laugh, facing yourself in the mirror like that pretending to smooth out his invisible clothing, and your laughing scares you, makes you think that maybe you have roused the Fates with your horsey snorting.

Mostly you just let the words, Okay, okay, okay, roll through you like a marble, the smooth glassy coldness finally lodging in your narrow throat. But you sit down hard on the panic that threatens to blow like an overstuffed suitcase. There are only so many ways he can put the words. He is not a fancy man. He once called a pair of short lovers a couplet, but that was a long time ago. You imagine he could say in the quivering voice of a treacherous Columbus: I have found someone else. And this sudden finding, this accidental discovery will remind you of things lost, then found, between the crusty cushions of a sofa. You know that one day the dictionary might reveal that "to discover" might actually mean to know more deeply, instead of this sudden coming upon, a chance landing, a lucky encounter of any kind. This world is crowded. There is bound to be a lot of banging and tripping, but that doesn't have anything to do with real knowing. And if he chooses these words, you will think: But I am hidden, too. Find me. As for him, you cannot even imagine what his rituals are, how he manages to protect himself against you, what lonely trinkets he carries with him just to keep the worst away. And all our spells, the words we do finally say aloud, are confusing and dangerous—I love you and only you—as though this were a good thing. Words are starving you, making you skinny with their veiled sustenance, like that graffiti that is sprayed across the alley wall: *Don't Eat Fast*.

* * *

A million things die in a day: the flowers in the vase; the thoughts on your tongue; the momentary moods; the flies trapped inside the window panes; a spider in your sink; cells; the wind; another day; all these things. Nothing is ever over and done with for good. You'll never eat enough to be full forever; the dishes just washed will only get dirty again. We celebrate and mourn in extremes. Only marriage and that strange rewinding of divorce. Only birth and the queer familiar nightmare of death. And over and over again we still have nothing to say. At your wedding no one talked to you. As you passed by in your short silk dress some women called you skinny, but your friends stayed drunk and detached, and in all the pictures they are smoking and look angry. And not a single fairy was brave enough to touch you with her bony finger and warn you that in the years to come you would prick your finger several times and fall down dead, and when your dry dusty kisses could not save each other you would have to slough your scaly flesh; and which one of you would be strong enough to sit the vigil until one of you might smell the mossy regrowth of your skin, the fruit fuzz of your new bodies? Well, what did you want? he asked, scraping your back with the fancy loofah that night in the hotel room. From midnight until morning it was all water games, moving back and forth from the giant shower to the deep round tub, steaming, soaking, cooling off, parboiling like vegetables. Something about the water and the dark room, and the still lake of the tub pulling you under, your newly heavy finger weighing you down like rocks. Submerged to your eyeballs you stared across at him like a frog, thinking that if this never starts it never has to end, thinking that neither of you was frightened enough, that except for stage fright there was not enough horror, that there should have been blood-red masks and beating drums, someone should have shaken a skull in your face, asked for some blood, wrapped you in snakes. You should have been able to dance your most horrible dance for him, your dress torn from your body, the whites of your eyes spastic and furious. The women should have beat their breasts, the men should have gotten down on their hands and knees to howl like wolves. In all the pictures you are smiling too widely, and your gums look raw and swollen. I wanted to sweat more, you tell him. I thought I'd be hotter. I wanted it to feel like a fever.

* * *

Your daughter is writing you love notes. You find the crumpled beginnings under her bed: Dear Earth Mother; Dear mystical wife; Dear Nile queen; Amazon lover; Two-legged wonder. You are proud of your sorceress, the way she takes it upon herself to do the magic that needs to be done. Still, you think you might have taught her that there are some moments where it is best not to be swayed by just words. And then there is the sad way we make our children hold everything together as though they were some kind of embalming fluid. How to tell her that you really believe that second chances are the real afterlife, but that you need that bone-scalding feat, that wild deadly stampeding in your heart to pass through the initiation over to the other side of living. In her room you find her copy of *The Egyptian Way of Death*. You remember her brief fascination with mummies, the way she would recite sections on how best to keep bodies as though they too were poems: removal of the brain, evisceration, first washing of the body, stuffing of the body. You open the book and read where she has underlined in red: "Special care was taken with the heart, which always had to be left in place. It is still to be found in most mummies, and though it is sometimes damaged by the embalmer's knife and sometimes grazed or gashed, it is invariably in the normal part of the body." You only hope that this could reassure her that despite all your nightmares and phantoms, your heart is actually in the normal part of your body. Once your man took his daughter to watch an autopsy on an orange cat that died from a fat, clogged heart. She watched her father rip through the rigid thorax and swore she heard mewing, but it was only another hospital cat moaning from a de-clawing. Could that really be her father, his sleeves disappearing there inside the cat's chest, pulling out organs, his hands covered in blood? It was just after that that the embalming book appeared in her room, opened to the picture of a stone sarcophagus in the shape of a cat. It is also the year that she practices holding her breath and makes you count the seconds she can go refusing air. It's the stillness, she confides to you one night. That subdued silence where all there is is the drumming of your body beating in your temples, where everything stays the same until you feel you're about to blow. She is practiced at this deception. Sometimes when you feel everything is fine, you look again and realize that she is not breathing.

Your daughter finds you in your studio filing the fine tip of a wooden spear. She touches the things you have made by hand: knives with strange carvings, poppets, brooms made from blackthorn or willow twigs, garters, crowns, silver half-moons, goat horns and drums. She takes off her shoes and the sawdust from the floor coats her sweaty feet. This month she wears red: tight cotton leggings that stick to her long limbs like the fluids— blood, birth, abortion—all running down to her small bony feet. When there is nothing doing, no weapons or charms to be made, she sits with you and memorizes poetry. She read somewhere that prisoners and torture victims could keep themselves alive by reciting all the poetry they remembered, and ever since has made an effort to arm her private arsenal with words that might save her life. Today she brings word of the man she has named the Mad Rapist Killer. She names him like a cartoon monster, as a way to contain him, as though he was the only one and after him there would be no more. She gives him a name, a proper noun, but the police call him a subject, something you might take in school, something that always comes before the verb, verbs like "to slaughter," "to strangle," "to butcher." They give a fair syllabus for all who are interested. They say: The subject is Caucasian. The subject should be considered dangerous. And the experts are calling it ritual murder. She touches a stone carving, turns it over and over in her own etched palms. But before she can pocket the rock, take it like a talisman, before she can tell you that she is not afraid of anything, that she sleeps in her own bed now alone for a while, before all this, you carry her out to the night to claim your block like dogs, like bitches or queens, raising your tails, rubbing up against trees, sticking your face into bushes, knocking over garbage cans, making her bark: It's my world too! She is reluctant at first and then quotes for you: *"Beware, beware, blah, blah blah, and I eat men like air."* She grows in spurts, your little witch, a faucet turning herself off and on. One moment she is timid, nodding her head politely to the night moon, a horrible habit she must have learned from you, that good manners might keep her safe. You do not want her to be this twelve-hour woman, this Arctic summer, this inverted vampire that night cannot enter, who gives up her blood instead of asking for it. And then she is something else, singing with you an improvised off-key dirge, howling: It's my world and I'll cry if I want to, her legs wide and powerful like a jockey's, her whole body, her ass to her hair, bouncing and shivering like a race horse. She is animal and rider, one powerful, snorting beast, her nostrils wide, taking everything in, and in your new world there is no room for rider and steed: it is all one powerful monster. She puts her lanky arm around your waist and asks: Is mankind an oxymoron? You tell her that as far as you know oxen are usually castrated and docile, and when she laughs and you see that she is about to tell you of her love, you cover her mouth with your cold hand. A public service announcement is pasted to the wall at the end of your street. It reads: We are all victims of child abuse.

* * *

Despite the gravity of the situation, the Head admits that the moon is his mistress. He loves her bald, cool body and no one can resist the press of sex, who photograph the Head drooling at the night sky, throbbing at the thought of something new again.

* * *

Your man is not going anywhere. This is only a small, natural death that you both misinterpret as the end, like clapping before the poet is finished, or calling rain "mean weather." But you will not bury these moments or pat them down with leafy silence in the churning earth. There should be passages for these mountains, a pass or bypass to make your brick heart bigger, and tents for the nervous travelers to rest in. Even snakes must have a place to leave their skins. And so in imitation of other passings, you sit your family down to the feast of the Death of Passion. You lift a wine glass to the man and say: To the regrowth of our flesh. You eat root vegetables with herbs and crisp bread with dripping cheese, things that remind you of the pungency of sex and the crustiness of bed. He wipes his mouth that is stained by beets. He begins: I am dead to you because I am not a poet. I am dead to you because I have never cried. I am dead to you because I have refused to read your mind, to give you what I know you need. I am dead to you because I confused giving with giving up, and what I thought I had, I halved. You tilt your glass and spill the wine drop by drop on the white cotton cloth. You say: I am dead to you because, like God, I tried to make you in my image. I am dead to you because I idolized and then got bored. I am dead to you because I gave you fences and borders and then pointed my weapons. Your daughter watches her parents die but she is undisturbed. The bodies still look so lifelike, and the hearts are all in the right place. And she writes you only one more note in a script that looks so much like his that for a moment you are forced to wonder: *I'll talk. I'll talk. I'll say anything you want.*

For seven days there is mourning and you speak of each other only in the past. I never knew your mother practiced my leaving, he says to his daughter. I never knew your father dreamed in color. With you, says your man to the ghost, all I wanted to do was sleep. Without you, I cannot sleep at all. I never realized, you say to your phantom man, how often I closed my eyes when you spoke. Your daughter dusts your photographs and pretends to cry. One day, in your dark, silk pocket you find the beginning of something, just a few words quickly scrawled in your own handwriting—the sad-eyed bride—and you wonder if you've only been fooling yourself. Meanwhile, the highways and city streets are full of new signs. A shoe company puts up a billboard that says: Just do it. A camera company shows its power with a great zoom lens and the words that say: Just shoot it.

* * *

This happens before the music is composed, when the players can't decide if they are going to go major or minor, and when the war remains still unnamed. On the longest night of the year you tell your new man to put on his iron long-johns and follow you out to the wild. You drive to where there are still trees left and go out in a weathered canoe to find yourself two small islands. After your great dying, little green buds of knowing appeared on your winter bones, and in the silence of your mourning you smelled life coming at you like heat, musk, and animal sweat. Your daughter sits between her ghostly parents who have died and come back unafraid. Your man steers his Mad River canoe, and the delirious cries of the loons make the lake a strange asylum. Your family sits like quiet Indians, the dogs keep a watchful eye for shore, and just the sound of the paddles breaking the water stirs the stillness. You leave your daughter at a small rocky island in the middle of the lake. The dogs, loyal and sharp as wolves, want to go with her, but tonight she is alone. The dogs watch her disappear, barking after your girl, who is leaning there against that twisted tree (the only thing you really saw before you turned away), barking as she fades to such a brief smudge that some hunter with bad eyes might wonder, Is that an animal? You do not go far: another island just across from her. If only you were wolves, you think, as you and your man pull the boat up the rocky shore. It could be so easy just to shake her by the tangled fur, her scruffy neck, to teach her courage and freedom, to give her the great earth as a home and a howl to match it. Tonight she is the initiate. You made her tools by hand and wood, a string of glass beads to see her through the night, but that is all for ceremony, props for a ritual, and the rest is up to her. You set up camp, the tent, the fire, and turn circles on your small land to see if there is anything else to do. This need to keep busy is an infection; your hands begin to tremble from emptiness, your mind sputters barely formed ideas in withdrawal. What did you ever do with stones and leaves, cold cold water and high unclimbable trees? You do not know what anything is called, not the names you've given it all, or the names they've given themselves. You know only the words for travelers: leaf, mosquito, crawly thing, dirt, spider; something slimy. But nature puns and jokes and you are just not fluent enough to hold a conversation. The dogs have made it from one end of the island and back again. Burrs and seeds catch in their fur, and they eat small blue fruit from a low branch. Their mouths hang open; surely they are laughing. They do not get bored or disenchanted. Everything they do is as though it is for the first time. It is already dark, and still you do not see the light of the fire across the water. You think of bears, though you know it is unlikely, but you force yourself to stand it and think: Let it be bears then. It would be an honor. She has a strong life force; it is right that you ask her for it. Your man has finally agreed to be your empath. He holds your head in his hands and his fingers smell like smoke. He says only: Howl.

On a flat rock that juts out over the lake you howl with your man, in loneliness and jubilation, in greeting and in fear. The dogs join the barking, and the whole anxious chorus sounds like a pack of many more than four. You watch and howl and think of matches and dry wood, sudden flames, deep embers and easy winds.

Finally, a small glow, a little orange star appears on the island, winking at your restless pack that stops you all dead in mid-howl. You imagine that she is reciting the poems to keep her safe (maybe: *out of the ashes I rise with my red hair....*) You imagine the warming of her fingertips, the singed smell of her hair, the bonfire smoke in her clothing, the smell of the phoenix; you can almost see the white glint of ash flapping through the air. The dogs lie down to sleep. Your man holds your firm hand.

* * *

And somewhere else a bored, unshaved Head imagines that he is the burning bush that won't consume itself. He holds his lovers in a necromantic embrace and tells them not to move. He is disturbed by the sound of his own heartbeat and wears thick sweaters to keep it muffled. People insist that there are ghosts in their midst and that they can see right through them. Their hands pass through their bodies as easily as reaching into a cold, clear stream, but they are too well trained and refuse to believe their eyes. An architect studies the neatness of cemeteries. And a zookeeper swears he hears the sounds of sawing in the night. At the entrance to the national park is a cardboard moose that everyone mistakes for the real thing. They snap a few too many pictures before they realize their mistake. A great buck, his thick velvet antlers rising high above the bushes, passes unnoticed behind his decoy and disappears into the forest forever. But probably these are only ghost stories that hunters tell in a loveless season, about the ones that got away, the ones that disappeared into the green eyeball of the forest, the ones that refused to be had.

The Last Ferry
by Jennifer Mitton

It was an odd, muffled sound, mechanical yet unsteady, like the bell and spring of an old Olivetti releasing its carriage at startling moments or every time you struck a certain key. The sound grew louder as she approached the terminal.

Across the river the mountains had fallen behind heavy cloud, and even the nearest trees were pale, their trunks silver with disease. It was early November and mild, but the leaves had fallen and the birds were gone. There was nothing at all to flutter.

Perhaps the last scheduled ferry had been canceled; the lot was empty, and the ticket booth appeared to be closed. Then she saw movement. Deep in the ferry walked an erratic figure carrying a light.

Pearl had come to see a doctor; she had come through dark rain and traffic and got lost. She would ask the ferryman for directions.

When she reached the ramp he was gone, and she waited with the heater blowing against her nylons. Her windshield wipers gave the dark scene life, and she prayed in time with them: "God watch over us as we in our nightmares sob, for I in my nightmare dreamed that I did kill, that I would kill again."

Then through the gloom the ferryman appeared, moving across her vision with each sweep of the wipers. When he came into the path of her headlights she saw that he was walking quite steadily; only his flashlight waved like a drunken impulse. He was about to disappear into the darkness again when she honked.

He turned, and his flashlight found her car and fixed it. He made an ambiguous sweeping gesture of invitation, then resumed his course. She started her car and drove in first gear toward his bobbing light. Before she pulled up beside him she swallowed her gum. An old reflex, even though she knew teachers chewed gum and fathers did not always provide.

He waved her into one of the lanes and shrugged to show it didn't matter which one. He smiled as if he had a toothache. Already it was impossible to tell him she wasn't trying to board the ferry. Many of the chronically sick have faith in magical coincidences.

The last one had changed Pearl's life. It was one morning in early October, and many of the people waiting at the bus loop hadn't done up their jackets. She stood outside the shelter, chewing at the inside of her mouth while she looked the people over— one had worn the same pair of jeans for days, another seemed unusually cheerful. Suddenly she saw a man her father's age, a man who had her father's pink cheeks and weathered throat. She hadn't seen him for years, but in an instant she was sick with rage. Murderous rage, and then, abruptly, the urge to kill herself.

Her bus came. Even a lecherous man, a man of a certain age and stiffness of neck, needs to ride a bus, needs a job. Needs love and understanding and the company of his daughter, she told herself. She fantasized how she would carry out her suicide. Surely not with razors or with pills, and she had no gun. The urge was as ordinary as a gas gauge light coming on, a simple problem requiring immediate attention.

She had prayed. She was not religious, yet the words came from a part of her: "I have lost something God gave me. God save me," she prayed, "my air is so thin."

She did not kill herself, but went instead to see a doctor. She spent all of October and most of November seeing doctors, and not one of them gave her drugs, but this last one did give her a referral, he wrote "Ferry Terminal" on a pharmaceutical note-pad.

It was a relief to drive far across the city with her referral; her adolescent desire to commit suicide had long diffused, and now she was worried she would not be able to keep her job. Her telephone receiver had grown greasy with use. "Not next week," she told the receptionists at one nearby office and lab after another. "Today."

For this referral, the doctor had assured her, there was no need to make an appointment. She went straight from work the next day. Traffic stopped before the bridge; it was raining, perhaps there had been a stall. Why was it that so often when you were stalled in the rain or hunting through a file folder for an old receipt you felt sudden waves of blood, warmly rejected, waves no napkin could have held? How was it that so much of the tension in your adult life could come from not knowing how much blood there was?

The ferryman was still waving her on, and as she locked her car she saw movement ahead and walked toward it. (Chicks walk toward the first moving figure they see.) There seemed to be a line of figures in the shadows. As she walked through the damp darkness she listened to the mechanical bell, the Olivetti releasing its carriage again and again.

The figures were indeed in a line-up, some of them crouching, others stretching with their hands held high. When she grew close she saw the last one was naked. Indeed, she could see no further than the half-dozen before him, and they too were naked. They appeared to be huddling on a narrow ramp covered with straw; beside them a conveyor belt jerked by with quiet but insistent anarchy. This was the old Olivetti, and when the bell rang the belt moved ahead.

There was something warm and familiar about the line-up, or perhaps Pearl had been feeling terribly cold. As she took her place behind the naked man, she felt a wave of steam so hot it took her breath away. Seconds after she had recovered there was another wave, and another, and finally there was nothing for it but to pull off her clothes, though she knew if the waves of steam were to stop she would freeze.

She was a part of things now.

Through the steam she heard coughing, the sorts of coughs she had never had to fear; she thought of tuberculosis and smallpox, influenza and diphtheria, and from each one she felt a warm, threatening breath bathe her naked body. They made child's play of her own complaints of twitching muscles, insomnia, dizziness and sudden internal pains—her surrogate-suicide symptoms.

The coughing directly ahead became irritating, and she fantasized about clean air ahead lower down, closer to the river. Then she saw that the overhead pulley system was designed to lower the whole line down, on an angle, so only the front half would be submerged.

It would make sense to lower the front end first; surely it was a kind of natural law. But if the front end went down, the rear would have to be lifted still higher into the cold; should she safeguard the clothes that lay beside her, gathering dampness?

Thinking this over as she stood in line was like being in grade school, comforting and frightening, the possibility of being right and a bit wrong always with her. At last the ferryman came by, and she called out, "Sir!" and asked him how things were supposed to work. Had each person been summoned to this ferry? Why were they naked and standing in line?

"You'll want to move up when it's your turn," he said. And then, as if he wanted to soften it, "Usually a lot go out on the weekend."

Pearl began to smell their diseases and realized that their cowering posture and nakedness were the least offensive of their symptoms. The young man ahead of her, chalk-colored, smelled of rotting meat, and the leprous woman before him of the worst urinal sprayed with heavy floral scent. Pearl could not imagine how she would last, and her clothes, she saw, were now soaked, and covered with a sort of molted fur. If only she could faint now with disgust.

The belt beside her had been moving steadily, carrying nothing, but now plates of fresh food appeared, rolling past with each muffled ringing of the bell. Ahead she saw arms reaching out, but Pearl could not move. She studied the different foods and the man ahead of her and tried to guess which plate he would select.

She saw he was a young man—perhaps not yet twenty. Steak and fries? A many-layered sandwich? Astonished, she saw him reach for a dish of sliced cucumbers, and now the smell of vinegar marinade was strong, and all at once she was in her place at a smooth white kitchen table, eating her fifth or sixth slice, the sun coming through the window in a warm bar that did not quite touch the dish of cucumbers. The dish was Mel-Mac, and moments earlier her mother had wiped it at the dish rack. It was blueish in color, light but solid, nothing like the sky or any other blue she could think of. Beside her was her glass of chocolate-flavored eggnog, untouched, because something about it, the smells mixed together, perhaps, always made her throw up. Her teacher had been sick in the morning, and she wondered if she would be sick again in the afternoon or if she would return; with the substitute no one had been allowed to work on the space mural, and the substitute did not know how to do music.

She considered not breathing through her nose while she drank the eggnog. It was nutritious, and her mother would be angry if she didn't drink it. But for the moment her mother's back was turned, she was wiping the cutlery, and there was something savage about the way she let each wiped utensil crash into its tray. Pearl had an inspiration. The bathroom door was open; the sunlight danced on the sink. She wouldn't use the sink, the eggnog would leave a scum. She stood, suspended in her excitement, and then she heard her father's steps on the back stairs. The screen door snapped, and then he appeared in the doorway, surrounded by a cloud of frozen air and sunshine.

Pearl hadn't given him a thought since he left the breakfast table, when she saw her mother tilt her face up from spooning out porridge to kiss him goodbye. Now he was breathing all over the room, infecting it. Everywhere Pearl looked, there he was, still smelling faintly of aftershave and hair tonic.

She slid back into her place.

She waited until he was seated and served. She waited until he had taken several spoonfuls of his soup, buttering slices of bread and eating them in wide, wasteful bites.

She raised the glass to her lips, then brought it down again. "May I please be excused?" she finally whispered.

But her father said, "Drink your eggnog, it's delicious," and his anger vibrated all the way to the middle of the night. Then Pearl knew she was causing the bloody and terrible silence of her mother's beating, that her mother's bruises and damaged hearing were not sufficient. She knew she would have to offer herself up to her father in payment.

This memory faded and the conveyor belt came back into focus. Pearl watched tantalizing art supplies go by, neat and bright in their unopened boxes. Here and there were ordinary school supplies like the ones she had used as a child, clean and appealing. Even the stacked pink erasers needed affection, asked to be chosen. Pearl pressed her lips together, and the old Olivetti went "ping" and carried them on.

There was an interval when nothing came by. Pearl's body was coated with sweat; her scalp began to itch. By a wonderful coincidence the next items were pints of beer, a steady line of them, bubbling and cool-looking in their frosted glasses. The boy ahead took one and drank long, and Pearl needed no better advertisement. She too took a glass, and drank until the rising tang of bubbles stopped her.

Immediately she felt a wave of dust. She sat on an old flight of stairs and fire escapes on a street she had lived on in Montreal, her first big city. With her was Luc, wearing his suede-fringed jacket. Luc drank from the brown bottle and then, laughing, handed it to her. She felt her full breasts, the nipples hard under her second-hand sweater. Although it was May, it was still too chilly to sit on the front steps without a coat.

The snow had melted all at once, and she and her roommate dragged the rug outside. Her roommate beat it with her hands with the strength that came from kelp and liver supplements and from being American. Pearl banged the broom against it, awkwardly.

She felt the dirty breeze lift her bangs: damp but still blonde as a password. Not such a bad memory! But as she sat, she saw her mother take this photograph from the letter, and with small, sharp hospital scissors cut Luc off. And she remembered herself, underneath him, waiting for him to stop his proud pumping. She had a longing, but it wasn't to bury her face in his flat brown hair, or to kiss his lips—lips that disappeared when he smiled. Then she saw her next boyfriend. Perhaps the longing was for him? Her prince.

She shut her eyes, but he continued to shuffle toward her, bent on his apology. Frantic to stop the memory, she reached to touch the coughing, naked boy ahead. His flesh was real flesh, and the instant her fingers made contact she smelled coconut and heard the roaring surf.

They lay, still naked, beside one another on the hot white sand. She saw that the boy's stomach and thighs were covered with open sores, and when she sensed he was about to roll over, turn to her, she groaned aloud. Perhaps this time she was allowed to faint, because it seemed a screen flew up instantly between them, and at her fingertips was an electronic console.

Select: Season/Weather was lit up, and instantly she relaxed into this soothing binary task. Ahead she could make out the boy's screen—he was alone now on his tropical beach—and she saw that others further ahead in the line-up were involved in different landscapes. Pearl selected *Spring, Warm and Overcast*, and for *Actors' Average Age* she chose *12-18*.

She pressed *Go* and smelled a wave of cypress-scented air. She was standing on her ten-speed on a suburban crescent, leaning over the handlebars and feeling the air on her back where her T-shirt slid up from her jeans. She watched her younger self turn to Joy Sanders. (Joy Sandwich, the boys called her, because she was thin, but there was sex in this nickname, and everyone worshiped Joy's long bones, her long black hair.) Pearl turned up the *Volume* and heard shouting from their friend Irene Sawatsky's house. Irene was getting permission to cycle to the mall.

Then Pearl saw another control: *Identification*. She turned the dial to *Closer* and was immediately filled with a restlessness she hadn't felt for years. Now she was leaning against jewelry counters, now prowling through the lingerie and sweaters and shoes and make-up, ducking past the mentally retarded security guard, and then, oddly, now she saw her boyfriend's ex-girlfriend—the one who had once declared at a dance that Pearl wasn't dressed well enough to get in. Through all these images she worried she would not be able to keep up with Irene and Joy on the hills. Irene was fat but strong, and Joy would dare anything if Irene wanted her to.

On her own, Pearl avoided hills. It was possible to take a route all the way to Poco with no hills, but the mall was further. You chose between the long hill the Port Moody way, or killer hills going past the asylum.

Irene and Joy had already stolen albums at the mall, and Irene had stolen a knee-length leather coat and modeled it outside the café on Friday night, her pretty lips frozen in a smile.

Pearl felt the ferryman's whiskey breath before she turned from the video. He reached across her and turned down the volume. "That mall," he was saying. "Was it up-scale?" He peered into the landscape he had silenced: three long-haired girls cycling toward a river, preparing to cross the bridge single file.

There was something about the ferryman that made her feel sick, the sickness burrowing through her insides and wanting to come up her throat. He turned *Identification* to *Further*, and Pearl caught her breath. "It was a suburban mall—families...kids...."

The ferryman nodded. "We didn't have malls when I was a boy," he said. He paused. "You're here to see the doctor?"

"Is there one? Yes."

"We have to run a check on you first," the ferryman said, and then, with the same grim smile, he turned *Identification* back to *Closer* and walked on, his flashlight bobbing from one landscaped screen to the next.

Pearl had never stolen. In stores she looked for what the popular girls were wearing, and sometimes there was the money to buy a top. Today she knew she was following Joy, whose parents had lots of money and who stole all the time. She was going to see how it was done. But now Joy had disappeared, leaving Pearl in the Young Ingenue section with her bra hook digging into her back, the sweat from cycling having brought out her new allergy to metal. She couldn't reach behind to adjust the flap under the hooks because the saleswoman was already watching her.

Before her were mohair sweaters, each shade filling a cubby of glass and metal tubing. The sweaters were soft-looking, like pastel hamsters. She touched a pink one, felt the saleswoman watching her, and picked it up. Then she took a cream one and the blue one and then a silver one, and a second silver one, quickly, as if such a wide range of colors might obscure the facts.

They were all tight around the neck. The silver one would look good on Irene. She could see Irene's eyes turning misty violet inside her black eyeliner, her sun-bleached hair flat over one cheek. But on Pearl the sweater looked plain gray, and her eyes were as usual, no, worse than the way she was used to seeing them in the bathroom mirror. "I have never stolen," she thought. She pulled her navy sweatshirt over the gray sweater and took her time browsing through a rack of blouses before she left the store.

Joy and Irene were eating hot dogs. "But we'll wait," Irene said cheerfully, with a sparkling hint of menace. Pearl was too jumpy to know if she herself was hungry, but she bought a plain hot dog and ate it quickly, sitting with Joy and Irene on imitation wood benches. Outside, the warm gray sky made her sleepy, and under her sweatshirt the mohair began to itch at the back of her neck. Her legs were tight from the ride in. I will never do this again, she was thinking, but already Joy and Irene were talking about coming back next Saturday.

Pearl remembered school a few years earlier: she had got a low mark on a science quiz and so could finally enter the club where you had to have bad marks, C or C- at best, but when she enquired, the standards had changed; now you needed a D to get in.

It began to rain as she passed the mental institution, and Pearl speculated about the extra calories this would make her burn. She was far behind Joy and Irene, but they were waiting at the turn-off.

"Did you get anything? You took so long, we thought you got caught."

Pearl pulled out a bit of gray mohair fluff. "It's like wearing a cat around your neck," she said.

The screen went dark, and the ferryman was beside her again. "That's not why you're here," he said roughly. "You were a kid. We didn't have malls," he said again. "We sat on the porch, and if we had a nickel we bought a big bottle of Coke."

He was still talking when she heard the first meows. She loved cats, and right away she was looking for kittens. A homeless mother cat might like it down here—there must be mice or rats. The ferryman turned away. On impulse she reached out, touched a bit of his orange jacket. "Let's say you belong to a group of unlovable people," she began.

But the ferryman said he had to move on. He left Pearl with her thoughts: if you belong to a group of unlovable people, grown up now, fatter and even more unhappy than when you were sixteen, nevertheless you must not commit suicide, your simpering lips must keep admitting you could get your hair done at an expensive salon, or for God's sake buy some cut flowers.

She was crying by the time she understood to whom this particular voice was addressed: it was to her mother. Why did you stay with a man who did not speak for months and years except in rage, a man whose movements were random and scarcely performed? It was the voice of women writing in their journals to complain about their mothers. It was her own voice.

She managed to stop the ferryman on his way back.

"And the worst for them was they had me," she told him, "a shrinking brat. Shouldn't I have hurled myself out the window?" The ferryman looked uncomfortable. "You might have written them some nice poems," he said. He was trying to remove a speck from his eye.

"Then I must be here because of my abortion," Pearl said boldly.

The ferryman looked blank, and only with his own voice seemed to regain his stride. "Abortion became illegal only in the nineteenth century," he said. "Efforts to legalize abortion have increased in response to population increases, pressure from women's rights movements, and a high maternal death rate from illegal abortions. Opponents continue to press for prohibition, but no one gets sent here for having abortions." He started to go. But Pearl held him back. She needed to talk about her abortion. "We were a couple new to our bodies' fire," she began, "our young-thorned bodies dry with thirst appearing, disappearing through the night." The ferryman looked sullen. "He always wanted toast," Pearl continued. "I would have made him a real breakfast, but he wanted me to leave so he could get to work."

The ferryman took a paperback from his pocket and, bleary-eyed, found his page.

"There was no plan for it: *abort* meant to miscarry, disappear, off, away, plus to arise, appear, come into being. I would not have enough to offer this baby. No father. Worse, a father who doesn't want to be a father. Who does not love the mother. And I, my little baby, I shook on my two feet, ever the unready." Pearl stared at the console, and its dark dissolved into a pork chop sizzling under a low ceiling, under a white plastic spatula melted in one corner.

There was no God for her. Nothing now was right. O Prince, are those your lips? She saw them pink and swollen. There were so many pink erotic things, and some ended in babies. Kettle on. Face washed. This baby would die. Nothing now was right, not the green color they had painted the walls. Mornings were at least more practical.

It was the day after the day he took her urine in. He got positive results, of course. He told her he thought all day about keeping it, but he got so scared, felt so useless. "You're so right for me and I'm all wrong for you," he said, and told her he had lain on the floor and cried. And staring at his weak face Pearl decided there was nothing to live for except other people's children after she murdered her own.

"I knew I would go mad," she wanted to tell the ferryman. But he was up ahead now, speaking with someone with more seniority.

At the time she had considered jumping on a plane for England, where she had a friend. There she'd be, in England.

She was alone and without God.

She walked into the clinic, the modern Church of Referral. She learned that her permanent would be relaxed from the anesthetic. At twenty-two, the counselor had already had two abortions and would have another. Large canvasses of acrylic female genitalia covered the walls.

Pearl did not want to be sold a code of conduct, was not

doing this for women; she just didn't have the good fortune to swell with her baby and croon. Perhaps she didn't deserve it.

"You're being pressured to keep it," said the girl. "But don't give up." She gave Pearl a referral.

Pearl found that when you are waiting for an abortion nothing happens. There is nothing to tell. She phoned nobody and wrote nothing and did not pick blackberries, no matter how many she saw. Afterward, she imagined the sheets dropped into boiling bleach, her own bloodstains thin and dull. Her thoughts returned, whistling past steel carts through the thickly painted hospital corridors. Leaving no traces no birds no singing anywhere.

"No, it was negative," she told her Catholic co-worker whose boyfriend was always offering, drunk at least, to marry her. "Probably it was stress."

What they did was bring the pregnancy to a premature or a fruitless termination. In morphology spines are aborted branches. We have morphologically sinned, you with your male breasts aborted teats, me with my empty result.

The practice of abortion was one to which few persons in antiquity attached deep feelings. Deep feelings of condemnation, failure of aim or promise, the empty result of any action, in other words our whole relationship, thought Pearl, each time she saw a baby, heard of another abortion.

The empty result was that she never tired of the empty result.

In the recovery room she cried herself out of the anesthetic. "If you are the doctor! If you can hear me! Please!" She in her nightmare learned that she had killed, would kill again. And was given orange juice in the name of the dead.

The cab driver could smell blood. He drove many women home, refusing to kill them though their despair made them beg.

Later, in her room, on her own again, then in another relationship, then out again, and then, and after that, the story always ends. There is nothing anyone can do.

A woman can miscarry without knowing she has conceived. Something mechanical out of control, the bell and spring of an old Olivetti releasing its carriage forever. The woman could be stirring noodles, or be stalled on a bridge, or hunting through a jammed file for some old receipt. At any time a woman may feel a rejection of blood. She must always scrub the streaks from her panties, scrub out the runes of waves no napkin could hold. Scrub and rinse until her fingers are ice and the water clears.

But you chose to miscarry! You chose to abort! Pay and pay the price! There in the line-up with the festering boy before her she prayed: "God I have miscarried something God-given, something God gave me, God save me, my air is so thin. The leaves do not flutter, the spruce does not complain. God watch over as we in our nightmares sob, as we in our nightmares learn."

The boy ahead of her stank. "These unlovely people," she told the ferryman, when he returned, "are people whose jeans have not been washed."

"They can take them off," said the ferryman, ignoring, as she had, that the entire line-up was naked.

She was praying, ". . . as we in our nightmares learn that we have killed and must kill again."

"You were kids. You were a couple of young people," the ferryman said.

"New to our bodies' fire," she agreed, nodding, surprised he remembered anything she had told him.

He was shaking his head. "It wasn't the abortion that got you here, it's the living ones you abandoned," he said.

Then she remembered the cats.

"No one comes in for abortion," the ferryman added. "It's things they've forgotten, things they didn't feel bad about."

Now she heard the meowing. It was leaving the cats. "I have been allergic to cats for years," she explained. But now she could see the cats she had left behind. After hatching, she told the ferryman, chicks go toward the first moving object they see. Did she bond with the cats or did they bond with her? Even now when she saw a cat on the street trotting through the mush of autumn leaves she called to it; she knew them all.

The ferryman listened. "So you left them with your father. You ran away, but you left your cats with him. You knew he would get rid of them."

"I couldn't stay with my father," Pearl said.

"You didn't want to?"

Sometimes you want to tell the truth so badly you would give up pleasure, you would give up all sensation. But all around her were stinking bodies, and what was the truth if you didn't know it?

The water below was violet covered with yellow oil. She wanted to be dead. Why couldn't she stay with her father? Because her father was crazy. Why couldn't she just be allowed to die instead of remembering? Her father fooled people—even now she needed multiple opinions, could not trust her own. His effect on her. He was inside her now, out of control. If she killed him she was the one who would die. She didn't want to think. She had a headache. She despised herself and wanted to die. "We don't learn from our mistakes," she told the ferryman, her mouth turned down with disappointment. "There's no reason to stay alive."

"Most people would have done the same thing," the ferryman said. "They would have left the cats." But his objection was mild; it too was part of his job. He showed her a form requiring her signature. It was near the end of his shift. He had nothing to live for; all he did was push people over the edge. "You are given one last chance before you sign," he said. He took a manual from his pocket, found the page and read: "Please imagine you are small again. You are in the bathroom. The adult in charge is about to drown the new kittens."

Pearl could hear the mother cat meowing. The kittens, of course, sounded like mice. She saw the mother cat circling around her father's legs. She was about to right the past! Never had she felt so good. But when she grabbed the kitten from her father, she saw it was missing much of its fur, and the soft bald patches were crowded with tiny black balloons.

"Ticks," the ferryman put in, and Pearl thought she might faint. The mother cat appeared with three more infested kittens.

"Are they going to die?"

"Of course. You shouldn't touch them," he said.

"If it's poison I'll be happy," Pearl whispered. But her jaws had come together. She could not reach out; and she could not open her mouth to speak when the ferryman asked if she'd be taking the cats along home.

The ferryman left her for several hours, but by the end she could no longer look at the cats. The boy in front of her was gone, in fact, all the people who had been ahead of her were gone. She was now at the head of the line-up, and below her was the violet water. "Please," she begged the ferryman. She said it through her teeth, because she knew now that he had always been her father. If nothing else, she prayed, let him do his job.

Letters (on a book lately circulating in the offices of Transport Canada)
by André Alexis

Let us therefore approach the question by reason.
 —Fridugis, *Letter on Nothing and Darkness*

After being inadvertently unfaithful to her husband, Mrs. Martha Williams of 123 Baffin threw most of her possessions away in disgust. Among these were seven letters from her cousin, Geoffrey Morehouse, a clerk in the Ministry of Transportation.

1. January 11, 198-

Dear Cousin,
 How are you? I am using my lunch hour in the spotted cafeteria to write you.
 I hope Aunt Lisa is well. Has she recovered the feeling in her hands? And Uncle Arthur? Are his nasturtiums brighter than they were last year? I know how much his greenhouse means to him. Since moving to Carleton Place, I see so little of my family. I am almost tempted to buy a car.
 Things are more or less well with me. Today I ate macaroni and cheese. There was nothing green in it, not even parsley. I was relieved. And it was a beautiful day. From the cafeteria windows I can see the snow-covered buildings and the blue sky. And there are skaters on the canal. They look like ashes.

Transport is the same as ever. They rearranged our floor again this year, for efficiency. Our cubicles are a little wider than they were last year, but not as wide as two years ago. Our partitions are a little more orange than they were and a little taller. The fluorescent bulbs are softer, and some of us have new typewriters. (Not me.)

My own cubicle is still in a corner. I do not have a window, of course, and I have only one neighbor. I do not miss company while I am at work, and the sound of other voices would be a distraction. And yet, despite my seclusion, I have lately caught a whiff of something peculiar here on the fifth floor.

You know, Martha, it would not surprise me if everyone in Transport Canada needed clinical attention. I am not certain I could tell the difference. The gossip around here is already so disturbed. I know more about Mrs. Weem's colon than I do about her. I have heard that Mr. Burton's wife left him for a woman, that Mr. Allard refuses to bathe regularly, that Mrs. Pirgic cannot control her bowels. (And yet, their hands are warm and their breaths smell of mint.) I feel so lonely knowing these things.

Anyway ... these last few days I have noticed that five or six of my co-workers have taken to reading. They are not reading their True Romances or Jacqueline Robbins. They are reading a leather-bound red book. Most of my co-workers are still reading the usual stories of carnage and carnality, but as I said, a handful of secretaries are poring over what looks like the Bible.

I suppose this means we are going to have another religious revival. The last one was led by Mr. Dixon, a born-again Hindu (believe it or not), and people on this floor kept things from India on their desks and quoted from the Bhagavad Gita at the slightest provocation. It is difficult to credit, but that revival lasted until Mr. Dalpy sent out his memo about incense at work.

How tiresome.

Yours,
Geoffrey

2. January 22, 198-

Dear Cousin,

How are you? I am using my lunch hour in the spotted cafeteria to write you. I hope all is well with Aunt Lisa and Uncle Arthur.

I am doing quite well despite today's special: spaghetti. I do not like it when the noodles are overcooked and the meat sauce is watery and tastes of thyme. I suppose this is why it costs so little, but even so, $4.50 is dear for a poisoning. I should not complain, though. I eat spaghetti at least once a week here, and it is never good.

Transport is the same as ever, really. I have grown used to the restructuring in our office. Of course, my cubicle is still in its corner, and I am still comfortably windowless. The days pass quickly.

I was pleased to receive your letter last week. It sounds as if you and Frederick are as happy as ever. And I am pleased you have decided to do something about the ants. You should not allow them to mar the comfort of your new home. (Still, how awful to discover an infestation. I would be wary of baths, too, after that!)

I have recently begun *Our Mutual Friend* and, so far, I am not enjoying the Dickensian run-around. I know it is your favorite, so I *will* persevere with the Podsnaps and Headstones, but I must tell you I feel uncomfortable carrying the book around with me. I think I mentioned, in a previous letter, that some of my co-workers had taken to reading a thick, red book. Well, even more of them have been reading it these days and, when they see me with *Our Mutual*, they assume I am reading their book. A few of them have been vigorously disappointed to discover I am only reading Dickens, and one or two have gone so far as to push the red book at me, all in the spirit of good will, of course....

And then, yesterday, I had a peculiar encounter with Mr. White from Accounting. I do not see him often, but Mr. White is one of the most pleasant men in Transport Canada: cordial, articulate, never an unkind word. But yesterday, by the water fountain on the sixth floor (where I had gone to make photocopies, our copier not working again), he came at me like a loon. Seeing my copy of *Our Mutual*, which I had brought with me, he said something very like:

"Oh . . . yes, very . . . Love the way it . . . Oh. It's not . . . Well, you should . . . Geoffrey, it'll change . . . yes. . . ."

I could not make head nor tail of it. It was as if sand had gone through the springs of a Swiss watch. It was the same Edward White. He was cordial and kindly, but he was completely inarticulate.

I did not make much of it at the time, but in the past weeks, Mr. White's has been a typical response. Everyone with whom I have tried to speak of the book has been just as inarticulate. Still, now that I think of it, he was the first who I knew to be articulate who lost his bearings after reading the book, and I find it odd that he, Edward White, should be inarticulate in exactly the same way as the others. Do you see what I mean?

All of this has actually roused my interest in the book. Is it a sacred text? Is it a course in grammar? A novel? No one has been even remotely able to tell me. They simply push the book at me, and, up to now, I have just as politely pushed it away. As of today, though, I will begin to trace the book's effect on the office. I will make a list of any notable changes in my co-workers. That should be interesting. (It will be difficult at this time of year, with the new budgets and all, but I am not a little intrigued by all of this.)

Anyway, please write. Let me know how things go with the ants, and give my best to Frederick.

Yours,
Geoffrey

3. February 2, 198-

Dear Cousin,

I am in the spotted cafeteria. My head is down, and I am writing you surreptitiously. I am not frightened, but I was lately reminded that discretion is a useful quality. I have been discreet in the past. I think it is wise to be discreet. I have had an unpleasant surprise.

I believe I have written you about the red book. It has spread through Transport Canada like a pox. It really has, and it really is like an illness. To begin with, there were Mrs. Adams, Mrs. O'Brien, and Mr. Flanagan. They are the first I remember seeing with their arms around the book. Then, there were Mr. Leonard, Mr. MacGibbon, and Mrs. Bonaventure. And, after that, if memory serves, Mr. White, Mr. Alleyn, and Frieda Morganstern. Since then there have been others (two of the janitors, for instance, and I must admit I was confused to see the janitorial staff reading), but it is no longer possible to keep track.

Still, the main thing is not their number, though their number is constantly growing, it is their behavior. It is not the usual thing. Not the usual thing with literature, I mean. In my experience, and you know how much I read, a book is, at very best, a way to moderate intellectual modification. One reads a book and, if it leaves a strong impression, one approaches the world in a slightly different way. (I myself was much kinder to animals after *Born Free*.) But, in my experience, it has never been a physical matter, a physically manifest change. I mean, you would not expect someone to limp after reading a book, no matter how good the book. And, what is more, you would not expect all of the book's readers to limp, even if it were possible for this book to give one of them a game leg. Each of us reacts to books differently. We react to the same book differently, in my experience.

And so, you can imagine how odd it was to discover that my coworkers, those who had read the book, have changed in small

but observable ways, ways that have nothing to do with my imagination. For instance:
1. They speak in fragments. (As though they were constantly overwrought. Overwrought buying cigarettes and coffee; overwrought peeling oranges, typing letters or drinking from the cooler on the sixth floor.)
2. The tips of their tongues protrude, whatever they are doing. (Up to now, the rest of us have been too polite to mention this, but I believe I am not alone in finding it unpleasant.)
3. They will say neither "I" nor "eye" (nor "aye" for that matter). (This is the affectation I most dislike. I first heard it from Mr. White, and then I realized the janitors were doing it, too. And, sure enough, I began to hear it from all of the book's readers. Last week I heard Mrs. Bonaventure talking about an operation on her "oose." Since then I've heard "oosight," "ooball" and "ooglasses." You can imagine my disgust. There is nothing I hate more than a verbal tic.)

I am not certain what these habits mean. They are more annoying than threatening. They may even be humorous in their own way, though it is distracting to look a man in the face when his tongue has not quite found its way back to the burrow, like a mole, snout out (Mr. Alleyn), like a squirrel from the knothole of an elm (Frieda Morganstern), like a rat from under a heap of leaves (Mr. Flanagan). Anyway, you see what I mean. It is downright peculiar.

Unfortunately, the pressure to read the book is becoming, just a little, aggressive. From their sentence fragments, I gather the book is "percutant," "fascinating," "brilliant." All I can see is that it looks well bound, and that is exactly what I tell them before I push the thing away. I have mountains of material to read, from the letters of complaint coming in, to the official apologies going out. I do not have time to read the book at work, and at home I am reading *The Waning of the Middle Ages*. Still, it has become inopportune to turn them down, now that Mr. Freedman, my immediate superior, has come in with his tongue protuberant, a copy of the book under his left arm. If he asks me to read it, what will I say?

Anyway, I am eating macaroni and cheese.

What has happened to your ants?

Yours,
Geoffrey

4. February 13, 198-

Dear Cousin,

Today I am eating in the spotted cafeteria. I have taken a late lunch. I am alone. The city is as beautiful as I have ever seen it. The snow has fallen for three days now, and it falls as I write you. From where I sit, I can see the Laurier Bridge. It is as white as your woolen sweaters. Even the cars are white. It is a day of falling snow and silence. I have rarely felt so sad.

I am eating macaroni and cheese, which I have not had for some time. Perhaps it is responsible for my mood, though I cannot imagine the cuisine here as otherwise than dull. That is part of the cafeteria's charm, after all, that and the view of the city which, on days like this, is like a view of my own soul, if you see what I mean.

Anyway, how is life? I was pleased to read, in your last letter, that Aunt Lisa has recovered partial feeling in her right hand. It must be a relief for her to feel some of the things she touches. And I was equally pleased to hear about Uncle Arthur's African violets. I can imagine his "restrained and enigmatic" smiling.

On the subject of the wingless hymenopteran, who shall otherwise be nameless, your basement must indeed be unusual. I can not remember ever having seen the little pests this deep into winter. I hope the stinking powder works.

Finally, thank you for your kind words about my "situation" here at work. Frederick's idea that the book is a sex manual is funny but, for all I know, he is right. No one has yet told me the book's title, and they are incapable of discussing its matter. The sex angle would certainly explain their loss of coherence, and maybe even the protruding tongue tips, but very little of the sex I have had has changed my accent. Perhaps I should have more of it with other people....

In any case, this morning Mr. Freedman insisted, in his inimitable way, that I "take this . . . take home, please. . . ." There was no way to push the book away without offending him . . . and so, I am writing you with a copy of the red book at my elbow.

At least now I know that it is not physically dangerous. I haven't changed after mere contact with it. Still, it is just as well I recently began a long, white book by René Belletto. It gives me an excuse to put off reading the red one, to carry something else around with me. If I read slowly, it may take as long as a week before I have to pick up the other one.

I hope I am able to read slowly.

Yours,
Geoffrey

5. February 24, 198-

Dear Cousin,

I am at home. From my bedroom window I see the moon over my neighbor's roof. I am not well, and I have not been well for a week. I know what is going on, though. A week ago, Mr. Freedman gave me a book to take home. You know the book I mean. It was not a work-related document, so I have had nothing to do with it. I have had nothing to do with it because I suspect it of being something other than a book. You know what I mean. It has clearly changed those in the office who have read it, and I do not wish to be changed. I am not often happy, but I would prefer to be miserable as myself than cheerful as someone else. So, I have not read it, but I have struggled to understand how it is possible for a book to do what this one has done, and now that I have had it near me for a week I believe I understand:

the red book is not a book at all. It is another mind. It is not another mind in the benevolent sense. It is another mind like a virus. What I mean is: if I were foolish enough to read the red book, I would become the mind within it. *That* is what has happened to the poor unfortunates at Transport. I know this must sound as if I had lost my bearings. It feels as if I had lost them completely, but I thank God I have finally understood the nature of the danger I'm facing: the loss of all that I've become. Someone is trying to un-Geoffrey me, or to have me un-Morehoused. Bear with me, Martha, I know this must sound peculiar, but I have proof. For the past week I have had the book on the night table beside my bed, and for a week I have had the clear sensation of sleeping with a man. (I do not mean sexually.) Though there is no weight on the mattress beside me, and no snoring, there is everything else: a vague odor of the body, a heat on the covers where he sleeps, a creaking of the frame when I am lying still. And how do I know it is a man? Well, aside from the sense I have of my co-occupant's maleness, I have lately been dreaming of a Norwegian man with an imperfect command of English. And every night it is the same: I am in a darkened room as a chandelier with wax candles gradually descends from an impossibly tall ceiling. As it descends, I see I am in a wooden room. The room smells of pine. And then, six feet in front of me, I see a thin and naked man with short, milk-white hair. Where his eyes should be, there is darkness, and his tongue has been pulled out at the root. How does he speak? He speaks with an eel he keeps in his cheek. (In other circumstances, I'm certain I would find this charming, but it is a sinister act in this context.) And how do I know he is Norwegian? His accent, the eel, which stinks of brine, and his only topic of conversation: Kierkegaard's teeth. (They're an unspeakably dull subject.) And, each night, I have kept utterly still, in the wooden room, while the Norwegian spoke of teeth and moved his hands before him, seeking me out. And how do I know he is seeking me out? Because as he was speaking of the Philosopher's teeth, he said "Are you there?" And as he was speaking of the Philosopher's tongue, he said, "I can feel you." For ten nights, we have been in the same room, six feet away from each other, and for ten nights he's chosen a different path through the room. He has not taken the same path twice. Sooner or later, however still I keep, and it is just as difficult to keep still in dreams as it is in life, he will find me. I have thought of moving away from him, but on the third night, when I began to lift my left foot, he heard me immediately and moved toward me. His teeth were white and the eel was in a frenzy, but I woke up as he touched me. (It was a revolting touch.) So, two things at least are clear. First, should the Norwegian find me, I'll wake up as someone else, as another of the poor souls at Transport. Second, I must do something about the book. It is a danger to me, but I can't bring myself to destroy something that belongs to Mr. Freedman. These people love their book so much, I have serious doubts about returning it unread, let alone in tatters. And, as you know, I have worked at Transport since 1967, over twenty years in the same place, moving slowly but steadily up, making a living my parents would have been proud of. In a way, work has been more of a home to me than my homes have been. I cannot risk offending Mr. Freedman. So, burning the book is out of the question. I have thought of reading selected passages, the title, say, and a few sentences from here or there, just enough to give the impression I have read the whole. But if the book's mere presence is so disturbing, what would reading it be? How do I know the knowledge of the title alone is not enough to destroy me? And if the title is dangerous, how much more so a sentence or a phrase? For all I know the typeface could kill me. So, I have had sleepless nights. Tonight, for instance, I am too tired to write, but I am writing to keep myself awake. The situation is intolerable. The more tired I am, the less I am able to perform my duties at work. (I suspect I am already drawing attention to myself on that score.) But work itself is the cause of my sleeplessness. Every time I see one of them with the tip of their tongue hanging out, it's as though I received an electric shock. I cannot relax. I cannot sleep, not even in the spotted cafeteria. Still, I tell myself I must be resourceful, plucky even. Perhaps all of this is not hopeless after all. I cherish the possibility that I am having a violent but temporary psychotic episode, that I am mistaken about the red book and the white Norwegian. But if this is a psychological derangement, I should seek help, but if I seek help I will have to speak of all this to a complete stranger. The thought is almost as humiliating as the Norwegian is frightening. And what have I done to deserve this? I have wanted only one thing from life: quiet. I have wanted quiet and a place to work in quiet and a home that was quiet. No television, no swimming pool, no fancy furniture, nothing elaborate. A simple place and a quiet life. I don't deserve my predicament. Maybe it is a test. But then who is the administrator? That's the question.

I am tired. How is my uncle's greenhouse? And what about the ants? Last night I had a vision of you and Frederick alone on Baffin Island, the world white save for the egg yolk sun and, at your feet, a brown anthill from which the insects crawled in such numbers the land around you was a black circle. You see what sleeplessness will do?

Yours,
Geoffrey

6. March 7, 198-

Dear Cousin,

How are you? I am in the spotted cafeteria. It is another cold day. The city is white; the roads are dark. It's all as it should be.

I no longer remember exactly, but I suspect my last letter was alarming. Your letter in response certainly alarmed me. I felt quite guilty having upset you so. It is at times like this I wish I had a telephone. (Frederick's suggestion that I use lithium was considerate, by the way, but lithium would have put me to sleep, and I didn't want to go to sleep.)

Also, I'd like to assure you that I am not at all "delusional," as you so kindly put it. There is a red book at Transport, and there is most certainly a Norwegian whose mind is the mind of the text. These things, which are really the same thing, have terrified me for months. They still frighten me. As well, it is an observable fact that my co-workers, all except one of the janitors, who is illiterate, and Ruth Kennedy, who is allergic to paper, all of my co-workers now share certain inexplicable tics: the tips of their tongues protrude, they mispronounce "eye," and they use fragmentary speech. The causes of my distress were genuine, but I was too panic-stricken to deal with them. It is my panic that upset you. I'm sorry.

Still, it would be hypocritical of me to downplay my condition. (Most of the hair on my back has fallen out, for instance.) And I don't want to give the impression I am completely out of the woods. As I write you today, I am carefully eating my macaroni and cheese, and carefully looking out the window at the city below. I am not used to eating with my tongue out, and that's only one of the problems I've encountered in the past few days.

Five days ago, I gave the book back to Mr. Freedman, unread. Since then, I have done my utmost to behave as the book's readers behave. It has been a nerve-wracking week. You can imagine the difficulties. I am involved in a tricky subterfuge, but this is the only way to avoid reading the book, to escape the Norwegian, to belong again as I used to belong.

The easiest thing is keeping my tongue out. I still have to think about it, but when I wake up in the morning I stick the tip of my tongue out. When I leave the office at 4:00 in the afternoon, I retract it. It is embarrassing to be seen with my tongue out. Two days ago, an older woman pulled on my coat sleeve and cursed me. She was so indignant. And, just yesterday morning, a young man tapped my shoulder to ask directions to Billings Bridge. As soon as he saw my tongue, he backed away and moved on. I suppose I could keep my tongue inside my mouth until I stepped into the Transport building, but as I sometimes meet my co-workers on the way in, I think it's safer this way. Besides, I have taken to reading the *Citizen* in the morning. I hold it close to my face as I ride the buses.

I realize it is dangerous to pull my tongue in at 4 o'clock, but by then I'm usually too exhausted to keep up the charade. Also, I have taken to holding a hand over my mouth until I reach Carleton Place.

The most difficult thing is to deliberately mispronounce "eye" and "I," or to avoid them altogether. It's not that I have much occasion to speak while I'm at work. I sit in my cubicle and correct the correspondence going out. Entire days sometimes pass with me at my station, head down, underlining, crossing out, checking spelling and changing grammar. Were it not for lunch, and the little demonstrations of *esprit de corps* expected of you, this mispronunciation would be no problem at all. As it is, it's complicated, and it's humiliating when I'm speaking to those who don't work on the fifth floor. (I'm not convinced my accent is any more humiliating than the tip of my tongue, but still . . .) And then, as if to make matters worse, Mr. Addison on the seventh floor lost an eye while skating on the canal (hockey puck). The day I spoke to him, three days ago now, he was still wearing an eye patch and he had with him two glass eyes of almost identical blue. He had to choose between them. Unfortunately, I was at the seventh floor photocopier with others from the fifth floor when he asked me which of the glass eyes looked more realistic. Years from now I'm certain to look back on all this with humor, but my effort to tell Addison that the robin's-egg blue was closer to his natural tint . . . it almost killed me. I maneuvered around the various "eyes" and "I"s. I was virtually incomprehensible for a full five minutes while trying to give the impression of being lucid and at ease. In the end, I think Addison thanked me. In any case, he didn't let on he noticed the slightest peculiarity. All I can remember saying is . . . Addison . . . Addison's oos . . . blue . . . robin's-egg blue . . . over and over until it seemed to me any normal human being would have had enough. And it worked. It was as if I had always spoken this way, with my tongue out. He thanked me; I'm sure of it.

It goes without saying that speaking in incoherent fragments is difficult but, really, I am so self-conscious now, so nervous about the impression I make, I rarely make sense in the company of others. (This, too, has made very little difference in my dealings with co-workers and supervisors. I'm beginning to wonder if I ever made sense at all.)

Anyway, today I've bitten my tongue only twice. It's a victory of sorts. And, in celebration, I have allowed myself to write this letter, here in the spotted cafeteria where I'm unlikely to be spotted. It feels good to write full sentences like this, as though the whole of the English language were moving beneath me like a river. It feels good. At least there's one place the book hasn't touched.

I've just finished the last elbow of macaroni, so I'll say goodbye for now.

Yours,
Geoffrey

7. March 18, 198-

Dear Martha,

How're you? I'm using lunch hour to write. I'm in the spotted cafeteria, of all places. I hope all's well with you and Frederick. And I hope Aunt Lisa's recovered from her fall.

I have the feeling you and Frederick have found my last few letters alarming. I'm sorry. I realize I gave the impression things were dire, but everything's fine, really. And it's business as usual here at Transport. I was going through an early mid-life crisis, I think, so I think I exaggerated some of the situation here. But don't worry about me, that's the main thing.

Yes, it's a little peculiar that everyone here at Transport walks around with the tips of their tongues out. But, you know, when one of the mucky-mucks from Energy, Mines and Resources complained about it, I've got to admit I felt pretty annoyed. After all, who is Mr. Roger Dupont to come in here and complain? It's common knowledge we're more efficient than Energy, Mines and Resources and, anyway, I feel a lot less embarrassed by the tongue matter than I used to.

I feel comfortable, now, mornings on the bus. People understand I'm from Transport Canada, I think. And I admit I feel a certain pride.

Also, believe it or not, it's easier these days to say "ooh" instead of "eye." Who says it has to be pronounced "aye" anyway? And, it being arbitrary in the first place, who is Mr. Dupont to criticize the way we speak? Is Energy, Mines and Resources going to set the rules for inter-departmental communication? What gives them the right, if you see what I mean?

It's true all's not *exactly* as it should be. I still haven't read the red book. I feel as if I know something about it, though. And I feel it would be good if I could read the book. It's such a small thing that keeps me from my peers. After all, what is a book? Pieces of paper, page after page of words, strings of letters and conventional markings. Where, in all that, is a "mind" to hide?

Still, a few days ago, I had decided to glance through the book, to look through it one word at a time (at work, of course). I was clever about it, too. I cut a small rectangle in a sheet of black construction paper, so I could control exactly how much I saw, and then I borrowed Mr. Freedman's copy. Well, I couldn't get past two words of the title (I mean, of course, I only allowed myself to see two words. The words were in bold face. For all I know, they're the only words in an otherwise blank book. If it comes to that, they may even be the author's name, but I couldn't get beyond them):

NORWEGIAN ROADS

The only other thing I saw, as I closed the book, were pages filled with numbers. In the state I was in, the numbers frightened me almost as much as the words had.

I can't remember if I told you the dream I had about a naked Norwegian, but it was a nightmare, and for a moment there, wide awake at work, I was standing in a darkened room, waiting for the thin man to strangle me. After that, you can see why I won't be reading the book. Much as I'd like to.

Anyway, I'm fine and I'm doing well.

And I'm finished my macaroni and cheese.

Yours,
Geoffrey

Cerberus
by Rai Berzins

Vegetative symptoms someone was saying (I overheard) were a concern. In-law of some sort or other. I was in the office. It was just in passing. Vegetable land, you give it some thought. Vitamins, minerals. When this sort of thing becomes even less than scribbling, that I was an actual man at one time. Things most like memories that flicker and fade, not however with any detail by which you might firmly grasp them as yours, as from your life, your own. More like a movie, or dream (of course), but a dream you've no recollection having had, someone else's, or someone else's memory, which leaked out, which you've accidentally come across, which sticks to the brain like shit to a shoe. You'd think whatever memories you have would come at least from your own experience. You'd think so wouldn't you. You'd hope so.

Seemed something outside just now. Someone. I went to look but there wasn't. Phantoms, raccoons—"the possibilities are endless" (Spinoza? maybe or a wallpaper ad). Nothing on the tube again tonight (why I

abasia – inability to walk for which no physical cause may be found

abhorrence –

abjection – state of misery or degradation

abscess –

absorption – disappearance through incorporation in something else

abulia – absence or impairment of will power

acalculia – acquired inability to make simple mathematical calculations

accident(s) –

should think—). I got out the tapes I made in the winter February thereabouts. Remember I wrote you I'd tape the war? I did, or parts. Forgot though to label (how to label). Some of it at any rate, the first fuzzy days—nights—a blue ghost circus over Baghdad. Hot today, 33 C, the air like sour mud in your throat, you wonder what compels you to inhale. Strange how this desert looks almost inviting. A "dry hot" (not to sound insane).

Paul suggested his analyst. He means well, that's clear, one he leaned on when he made his voyage through divorce (not suggesting) and I took down the name. Konrad. More to please Paul. I told him if the word maybe didn't start with "anal"—but Paul says my problem's with money, or so he said his analyst said when he heard about me balking at the rate, or not so much money as the claim of concern over money when what it is (or might be) is a way of masking my fear of confronting my problems by way of an otherwise wholly commendable frugality (!). I had to laugh. I mean I would've, had I someone to laugh with. Someone not being analyzed. This is not a shot at Alice. I don't hate Alice. Whatever advice she gave you (?), whatever conclusions she "encouraged" you to draw—regarding us—is fine, and if it wasn't for that glimpse I had, that day I picked you up after the appointment, the two of you were leaving together—the building—were walking out—normal enough—and I thought who's that shrewd-looking woman with Muriel, "shrewd" was the word, she looks like a goddam rocket scientist or something—and then to discover the true nature of her work and her name being Alice and why I thought rockets, and then—or later—who is this person, this CRITICAL INTELLIGENCE, showing up on our shared path, like a fork in the road, but leaning your way, in the sense that she never got my position, she never got the other side of the story (I know it's not a story, not like we're antagonists (strictly speaking) but it's intimate, what goes on between two people, the intimacy), and having this stranger (stranger named Alice) suddenly there, her ear to those things you probably find too intimate, too compromising to divulge even to me, there's something—I don't think it's over-reacting to say I somehow found it something of a threat. "Intrusive bitch" was not the best choice of words. I realize now she was only doing her job.

Watching the bombs (strange, in retrospect, no longer swept along in the frenzy), to watch the bombs fall—the bombs being ours. Our side's. To sit at home. Here a bus stop, here a barracks, here a palace, here a bridge. Douglas Fairbanks nowhere in sight. Neither is Sinbad. Neither are you. Into my eighth finger of Scotch (ogre's fist), bathed in blue, the monochrome, the whisper of missiles, guessing Bali. Kuala Lumpur? 12 hr difference. Afternoon. On some beach, some sacred site. Paul says hi. We spent the

accouchement – delivery of a baby

acedia – laziness, torpor

acrodermatitis – inflammation of the skin of the feet or hands; can result finally in atrophy (see below) night in the faculty lounge, getting vague. I don't know if I believe in the brain. Said as much. Paul's assistant found this very witty, praised me no end. Wit should be met—if at all—with wit. Nothing worse for wit than praise. I didn't say this. Perhaps I should've. And if he only knew the source.

Mood-swings continue, whether due to the Ballantines (& aftermath), weeks w/o a letter, this being alone, or the ongoing strain of putting up with the stuffy stupefaction with which any of my summer session planning meeting motions are met. Try at least not to stink of the stuff when I pass through, which is less and less. Passed the Canterbury course to Paul. What it is about standing in front of a class these last few months I don't know. Had the thought of pissing my pants, in front of them, just for effect, to stand there speaking quite reasonably while the urine wandered its wide way down, to see how they'd react, if at all. And since the occurrence of this thought, I've lost a good bit of my concentration, it shifting instead to the sending of signals down to the bladder, the urethra, a firm but civil NO (tone is crucial). Managed an argument with Johnson today. It didn't take much. Concerning the war. You know that fierce clarity that comes sometimes? I went into the office (don't ask me why) this morning, four maybe five hours' sleep, mental limping, my throat like dust. Paul wasn't in (proof of his wisdom), so I found myself alone at the coffee pot. Johnson came over for water for his herbal tea, perhaps that's why, what struck a chord. I was suddenly saying how the bombing of Iraq, of the Tigris and Euphrates, had less to do with oil and tyrants than with wiping out the cradle of the Western world. This, in conjunction with the plan to redirect water from the Rockies, from Hudson Bay, to the Mississippi and LA badlands, would clear the way for America to claim that the "true West" rose up on the shoulders of American enterprise and ingenuity, a new river system which would run up and down, north south east west, the length and breadth of the continent, its name (what else but)—the America. Johnson scowled. He's got dual citizenship. He asked for my sources. I told him, the Unconscious. This didn't sit well. He called (as always) my nationalism blinkered, over-earnest, daft, my anti-Americanism paranoid and fuelled by self-interest and transparently hurt feelings at being passed over for Assistant Head in favour of that dolt from Pittsburgh (which I partially acknowledge). I hastened though to add that we—the Canadians—would not be excluded, we would have our role: as dam-builders, local labour, local colour, planners, advisors, and architects of our own demise. What is it when stern pasty men in tweed sip herbal tea and watch your lips? The man's the same goddam age as me, but he makes me nervous (maybe the booze), he

acrophobia – morbid dread of heights

Addison's disease – (no longer fatal)

aestivation – spending of summer (esp. Zool.) in state of torpor

affliction(s) –

agnosia – disorder whereby patient cannot interpret sensations correctly although sense organs and conductive nerves are functioning normally

agnosticism –

agony(s) – (general, specific)

is not "above" me, he's merely this resolutely drab authoritative thing that stands there, his own lips like two garden slugs making (if you'll excuse the term) love. I spewed all sorts of inanities—the list I'm making on what can go wrong, in the most basic sense, a catalogue of perils, conditions, distractions, that can stall/stun/cripple one over the course of the journey; why I want pencils, papers—all manner of recording devices—restricted from my classes; what he thought (it begin his specialty) of *Beowulf*'s Grendel being in fact a Sasquatch. The first two I might've gotten away with, but the third clearly struck a raw nerve. His lips separated, his grey teeth protruded, awash in camomile (meant to soothe). He turned away but in turning said something I didn't quite manage to make out. Fuck-you in Anglo-Saxon is my guess. Never utter it in English of course. Too new. Less than half a millennium. Still the taste of usage upon it.

8 p.m., still at the office. Going through papers, thinning files, a kind of purge—unsure through yet of what. The bulk, the terminal accumulation, the things you think that maybe somewhere down the line . . . Boxes and boxes and boxes and boxes. Very nearly forty minutes staring into one in particular. Nothing of interest. Just looking down. You see why the list. You think it's you—Muriel—who's travelling, who's gone away, is making tracks, consuming horizon with such great abandon. But

I'm the one who leaves as I sit, spiralling in darkness broken only by glimpses (too brief) of daylight and debilitating fits of cognition. I want the possible trajectories marked out, should it come that I have to "see" someone. Nice to know at least what's going. Gone. What seems now never to have been. Calm, equilibrium. Spoke with the janitor—George—mentioned the thing about Grendel. He liked the idea but thought I'd need bones. To make it fly. Of course he's right. He brought in some baklava. Asked my advice about a brilliant daughter. Rocket science I almost said. Analysis. But she's into the classics. I couldn't believe someone into the classics, that age, hers I mean, to be seventeen, to be thrilled by dead languages, somehow, anymore. I'm worrying now most about decorum. I almost want to take George's advice, walk in (where I'd get it I don't know) one day into Johnson's office, lay on his desk a three-foot-long petrified femur or tibia, say "Here's your Grendel" and leave. The wit is not the first to go. Hygiene maybe, nutrition, civility, but wit hangs around to the bitter end (perhaps not bitter, perhaps just ghastly—to me, one who's been paid by his brains, to have to come to terms with a mind unmoored, roaring on through dark, aware and incompetent, aware of just such incompetence —perhaps I'm biased, ghastly seems fit).

agoraphobia – morbid fear of public places, open spaces

agromania – pathologically strong impulse to live alone in open country

air embolism – air lock obstructing outflow of blood from right ventricle

akinesia – loss of normal muscular tonicity and responsiveness

Alphabet: alpha, beta—why on earth should it end at "z"—

alarmism – often unwarranted exciting of fears, warning of dangers

alexia – acquired inability to read

algolagnia – sexual perversion in which pleasure is got from inflicting pain on oneself or others

Thought I saw you on the street today. It was not you (rest assured) but I had to get within several feet to search out the details which made it not so. This woman talks, dresses like you and, Muriel, I swear—height, weight, hair color, nose—but the mouth is too broad, the hips a touch slimmer. I had to speed up, pass her, stop, and pretend to consider some overpriced oranges. She too was looking over fruit, looking up a moment, it was all I required. You know I thought she almost smiled, a sort of recognition, but it couldn't have been. I'd have noted the resemblance. I'd have—no. What the hell could there be to be gained—Hi you're the spitting image of my wife, I feel like I know you? No, I can't see it. (Thinking of the article Kay likes to quote, of all men being potential rapists due to the peninsula jutting from their groin (is this why I cannot talk to Kay?). Of course we are also potential saints, salesmen, and everything in between.) The thing is I did feel compelled to say something, approach her, I did feel this terrible draw. To study her, hang on her every gesture, follow her home (I didn't—I wouldn't!), only—only to see almost you, from a distance, before I knew you. To see you (i.e.—a version of you) as someone to whom I did not matter, could just as easily not exist. I looked back and she was gone. I'd bruised a peach, so bought it.

Paul's book finally came out, *Blind in One I: Re-Approaching Narration*, and they had a small reception in the lounge. I arrived numb and things went from there. Paul misquoted himself at length, Palliser passed out, Lydia left with a boy at work on his first moustache, and Johnson and I again locked horns. I said it was time for a movie of *Beowulf*, Arnold Schwarzenegger as the Geat. (I honestly do believe he'd do fine, the muscles, the accent that no one could actually prove was not Geat—besides, he doesn't say much.) Johnson flinched, but rebounded quickly. He asked who I saw in the role of the monster. I'd barely opened my mouth when Paul said Chamberlain—"Wilt Chamberlain, in moss." Johnson didn't recognize the name. We had to tell him. Can you believe it? What's the joy in baiting a man who swallows the bait and carries on regardless? I lost all interest and drank too much. I slurred. Johnson made some snide comment. I missed it, I gathered from Paul it was snide. I confronted Johnson, asked him whether—as I had it—he'd been snide. He asked was there a law against being snide. He would clearly neither confirm nor deny if he'd been IT with regard to me. I raised my voice, it seems I gave him something in the way of a small shove, a little push-off of my palm from his lapel. Werner

alidade – (lack of) instrument for determining direction

alienation – estrangement; a turning away or diversion from; (psych)1—experience that others participate in one's thinking; 2—insanity

alimentation – (lack of) nutrition, maintenance

alluvion – 1 – ....
2 – flood

Alzheimer's –
progressive dementia occurring in middle age

amaurosis – partial or complete blindness

amazement –

intervened and asked why I was angry. I couldn't—you know—precisely express it. The thing is Johnson did not seek redress, he knew his part in it, he got his coat and left. Paul was obliged to make the rounds. I killed some time in a corner booth, looking professional, pissed and perplexed, and could've remained there comfortably had it not been for Werner's voice, thick and insistent, him holding court with three of his students several feet off. These three could well've been sisters, not so much by looks as by gritty allegiance. Werner must've recognized a challenge. He plunged right into his favourite reminiscence of masturbating in the shallows off Tahiti and watching the little fish gobble his sperm. For whatever reason the three of them stayed, listening it seemed—can it be that it works? The lumberjack muscles, the Kerouac-quote tattoo. . . . Can it be that we're all so desperate for myth that we're willing to be blinded to be fed? I know you've always thought Werner an asshole, but how do these assholes get so often laid? I know we said we'd leave ourselves open ("open" was the word?)—to what, I wonder now. I'm in a corner. You're on some brink. I'm sitting with a glass between me and the world. Or was. Six feet between me and this student, close enough, even just to speak, to offer a hand out of the vortex of Werner's ego—in exchange for my own? My glass was empty, I'd been watching the one who seemed least enthralled by Werner's self-advertisements.

She was smoking and blowing the smoke out the side of her mouth with a kind of Popeye expression, and drinking Scotch or rye or something amber and straight enough it seemed to sting her tongue with every sip. She's taking notes, I told myself, she's standing there letting this asshole satirize himself—or satyrize (and probably would, could he bend the thing far enough around). She shifted and turned a quarter-face away from him, a third, a half, she was now as much in my sphere as his, and our eyes met, Werner's and mine, as our glances rode the wild terrain of that body decades younger than our own. Our eyes met and Werner winked, all the while keeping up the tale of his exploits, and I thought—you bastard—and made up my mind. I stood and as quickly sat back down. My glass in one hand, Paul's book in the other, I lacked a third to stuff in my pocket and redirect a sudden rising. The girl, oblivious to both of us, dropped the butt in the bottom of her glass, swished it about, the hiss more dismissive than any remark she might have made. She placed the dead drink on the mantel behind her, turned, and walked off and out of the room. Werner came to the end of his sentence, and one of the other two started in on Chatwin's study of Australian aborigines.

ambiguity –

ambivalence –

amblyopia – poor sight not due to any detectable disease of the visual system

Perhaps I've been misled by wit. Perhaps it *is* the devil's tool. Wit a weapon against faith. That there is no final joke to be gotten, for which we'd been grooming our wit all along. That the joke is on us, and not of the ha-ha variety, but sick. Sick in the extreme.

No mail today. Or the mailman came, brought coupons, flyers, unaware of the risk. I'd sat in the front room for 2 hrs 20, having awakened with the absolute knowledge that a letter from you would come today, knowing the earliest the mailman has come is 10 to 9 and I was there no later than a quarter to. Coffee, a head that's been brought up too quickly from ten thousand leagues below the sea. 2 hrs 25 mins later the mailman came and dropped off coupons. I waited till he walked from the door, till he was gone before I went to see. Going to see, I did not yet know there were only coupons, I knew he'd stopped, I'd heard the squeak and rattle and clump of the whole procedure. I felt somehow that if he'd seen me—before actually placing the letter in the box—if he'd caught a glimpse of my anticipation, my "need" for a letter, the "need" would pass from me to him, run down his arm, the selective acidity of the "need" being triggered by the discovery of the longed-for note, the letter would dissolve, the letter that might have been in his hand in the best of all possible worlds (which does not include parallel worlds, the companion world to the one of the letter, the world which did not contain such a letter, not today, not perhaps ever). The thing then is that no letter came, I checked the other boxes, I checked the one next door, I stood on the walk and studied the path between the buildings, the path the mailman habitually takes. He was standing talking to a neighbour two doors down. He didn't see me, not at first. I thought to approach him—but what to say—seeing his answer would have to be that if there'd been a letter he'd have placed it in my box. The neighbour was saying something about his "wife as a rule" doing this or that. His wife as a rule. If that's what he believes. I laughed, as much for their benefit as mine. They must've recognized in the laugh more irony than humour, for they turned and stared. I nodded and they both nodded back. O little town of Bedlam, I said—softly, to myself.

Held off drinking (in spite of the above) tonight until 6, tomorrow 6:30, maybe 7, till gradually.... Don't make me laugh, someone said on the streetcar today, several seats back. I didn't take it personally. To the best of my knowledge my thoughts have yet to actually start leaking from my skull.

ambush –

amentia – failure of development of the intellectual faculties

ametropia – abnormality of refraction of the eye

amnesia –

The woman went by again today, the woman who looks like you. She was wearing something like harem pants, slippers with the toes curled up, a vest, blouse, this you will see—you will see the staggering—in her arms, books, an armload of books, and

amok (amuck) – sudden outburst of furious and murderous aggression, directed indiscriminately at everyone in the vicinity

amourette – petty love affair

amputation –

dangling from one hand a see-through net bag containing fruit. I watched in a sort of stunned disbelief. I thought about that time in Vancouver, 1981 remember, when I swore I saw Lucky? Beckett's Lucky, Hemlock and 4th, something and 4th. Hemlock, Yew, one of the tree-names. Trudging downhill, toward the harbour. We'd gone out to get some acid for the weekend (acid one could trust), the guy didn't show, we didn't know that then, that he wouldn't, we were very much in a state of innocence. You stopped in a little store for trail mix, I stood on the corner, I was facing the harbour, and to my right, not five feet away, Lucky appeared, pausing at the lights. The pause went on through two complete traffic light interchanges, he hardly seemed to breathe. I thought, alright, he breathes through his pores. There were those around then who'd made it a career. The traffic resumed, which was when he veered out, right into it, through it, like it wasn't there. Everyone stopped, as much to stare as to stop their vehicles from challenging him. He was 6'5", in a suit for an overweight businessman of 5'9", with a bowler hat that had seen better days (what bowler hasn't), a suitcase bound with a belt and his pants secured to his hips with a rope. His eyes were blue (a bird's I remember), the pupils barely pinholes, irises you could swim in. Several days unshaven, thin grey hair to just past the shoulders, nose a wedge, mouth the scar of a wound long healed over. The breathing when it came was a wheeze, the smell a vaguely vegetable rot. Dingy white shirt w/o a collar, no socks, and laceless oxfords. It didn't take much to see who he was. You were still inside, delayed at the checkout, the clerk was trying to open the register with pliers. I stood there, caught between wanting to run after him, demand some speech, maybe rearrange his hat, that or haul you from the store, drag you along till you'd caught a glimpse. I didn't do either. I can't say I "regret" it. I stood transfixed. I thought blessed. My glance wavered back and forth between the two of you, you oblivious standing with your trail mix, Lucky now slipping in and out of the last sun breaking between the buildings. By the time you emerged, he of course was gone. You liked my story but that's all it was to you, a story about an uncanny resemblance. You managed to coax some mushrooms from Arnold, airport-field, later on when it became clear the acid-guy would not show. I passed on the mushrooms. You didn't understand. It's fixed in my mind, that struggle over meaning. I think you thought I was talking similarities. I don't think you truly grasped who it was I'd seen.

 Last night again the measured tumble (glass by glass) into furniture land. Watched to the end of the bombing tape. Followed by commercial, deals on cars. Had on the VCR for the tape. I scanned the dial, happened on a scrambled transmission of "I Dream of Jeannie" reruns. Put on "record" in spite of

anabiosis – state of reduced animation

anachronism – person or thing out of harmony with time

anasarca – swelling of legs, trunk, genitalia, due to fluid-retention

angina –

angst –

anguish –

(annihilation –)

anosmia – loss of the sense of smell

interference. Sporadic bolts jerking Jeannie back and forth across the screen, her perky good nature, taut cream tummy. Managed to freeze-frame on her bending halfway over to offer fruit. Spit in one hand, a sock in the other, my cock lurching up through the alcohol—it seemed the shadow in the satin crotch got even more provocative a couple seconds further. My thumb banged about (spastic with spit), fast forward to rewind to slow to freeze, again and again but it only got worse. When finally I let the fiasco cease, the image was Jeannie nearly erect, her arms as if paralyzed at her sides, her throat a grotesquely brilliant blue, the chest collapsed, the waist disrupted in a cross-screen slash of wicked light. My cock shrank, a tiny bauble of come at the tip the only suggestion of what had gone before. I fell asleep in the chair, and into fitful dreams, one in particular of being caught in a storm at sea. I get a hold of the *Moby Dick* coffin—Queequeeg's—but so it happens does Grendel. I'm thinking what if he tries to drown me, he has that look—but then there's commotion. Lucky and Frankenstein's monsters surface on the other side, struggling for handholds. We come to an agreement, we take a handle each. The sea calms as we talk. Frankenstein's monster has an "F" sewn on the front of his jersey, so we call him that. He's shy, sensitive, pretty well-spoken. A bit green, but then we all are. Grendel's hairy, but otherwise civil, and Lucky's as he was on the street. We all come from different walks of life, but all feel peripheral, so have that in common. Soon an island appears nearby. On it is a woman sitting in a sun-dress. She has a bottle of wine beside her. Has on sunglasses but I'm pretty sure it's you. She waves. I don't know whether to wave back, lead them ashore, in view of reputations. They tell me I can go alone. It's unclear though what might be in the water. I hesitate. It becomes a beach. Crowded. You get up and wander off. I check and find the water's only up to our knees. The others go swimming. They're magnificent swimmers. I open the coffin, which is now a trunk. In it are my papers, soggy and ruined.

Perhaps you realize I don't expect you back. Or would—you would, should you come upon this. As for the woman, was she a woman (on the street)—or was she a sign? The books—whose books? The fruit—indigenous to nowhere at all? Had I a telescope, had I more of that which does not come from books. FEAR RULES it said on some construction site wall I passed last night, so what is one to do? Make a point of confronting Fear, to let it not lead us into spinelessness? In every dog prepare to see Cerberus, hold all "development" up against the suffering of F, of Lucky and Grendel? It's just after 4 a.m.—again—the palace is quiet. Knowing some things, the TEMPORALITY of things, the thing of knowing nothing, of knowing merely that. This thing of thinking, when I look on this

antinomy – paradox

aphasia – disorder of language affecting speech, its understanding

aphrenia – failure of development of the intellectual faculties

apnea – temporary cessation of breathing

apoplexy – (see stroke)

apostasy – abandonment of faith, vows, principle, party

apparition –

apraxia – inability to make skilled movements with accuracy

later and it no longer means, of words not meaning—a thing, that I may well wake tomorrow and not know these words, or what words are. For now, maybe that I am merely me, and my name's Tom (or thereabouts), knowing full well one can't live forever, is finally finally left for dead, through no preventable "fault" of one's own, this Tom for instance this tom this man figure standing in the mirror, this tom named me attempting to somehow prepare to meet its god—

    TOM / GOD
    TMO / GDO
    OTM / ODG
    OMT / OGD
    MTO / DGO
    MOT / DOG

 Out the window the rain is falling—or more like something that has lost its way, is drifting down, a dense confused exodus from the sky, density increasing as it nears the ground. Streetcars gently press their way through, the odd cab, now & then a figure—

Two things that should perhaps be said—by way of background, significance. 1. Growing up, the most traumatic experience I daily endured was on my early-morning paper route. One of the customers kept three black dogs, large, loud and aggressive (those were not their names). She kept them inside ("as a rule"), but the mail slot was several inches from the ground, through which the paper was to be put, to the left of the door and directly below a sheet of plate glass 1' wide and 7' maybe 8' high. I'd almost always make it to the door without the dogs hearing, I would have the paper halfway through, when suddenly—always suddenly—out of the dim recesses of the corridor first one then the other then the other would appear. The width of the window made it such that no more than one of them could hit the glass at the same moment—so they'd rotate. The image was that of one huge body with three heads, all of which seemed solely bent on tearing mine from me. Our faces a foot and a half apart, separated by ¾" glass. 2. My favourite story at that time was H.G. Well's "The Door in the Wall," in which a man out strolling discovers, quite by accident, a door which leads to Paradise. But it's temporary, his visit is brief, and his life from then on is spent in preoccupation with the door. His life, from one point of view, is RUINED by this first vision which haunts him thereafter. The ending is, in the best sense, ambiguous.

The "figure" I saw from the window last night (or morning—however you care to view these things) seemed to be none other than the woman I'd described. She raised her hand—I thought at first a wave—to me—but in fact she was hailing a cab. I grabbed my coat and ran downstairs. Another cab was along shortly and the taillights of the first could still be made out

aprosexia – inability to fix attention on a subject

arachnidism – poisoning from the bite of a spider

arrest –

arthritis –

asininity –

asphyxia –

(**assassination** –)

astasia – inability to stand for which no physical cause may be found

through the thickening mist at the bottom of the street. We followed it as best we could. I described her to the cabbie as a friend who was leaving that day and had left with me by accident something quite essential. The driver asked if I didn't have the address. I said no, unfortunately. Friend of yours? he said with a tone. I said some people like to cultivate the mysterious, that it's no reflection of their integrity. He said, whatever, so long as I was flush. I placed a folded twenty on the dashboard and little else was said between us as we drove. Once or twice she seemed to elude us, but soon enough the taillights reappeared. He said he couldn't be sure it was her. I told him be strong and of good courage (after which he said even less). I suddenly made out where we were—a street adjacent to the old Necropolis. The lights on the cab ahead brightened with braking. I said to keep a distance. He didn't like that. He said maybe I should get out there, stopped, made change, a few dollars back, with little or no expectation of a tip. I said here's a loonie. He said "no guff." I hadn't heard the expression in years. I got out. He drove off without another word. The other car was still parked some ways ahead. The cab I'd been in, it pulled up alongside, there was some sort of interchange, then they both drove off. I saw what looked like the figure moving along the sidewalk on the street perpendicular to the one on which I stood. The pace was brisk. I wouldn't catch up without running, and thereby drawing attention. However, if I scaled the fence, took a shortcut through the Necropolis—which is what I did. Getting over was simple enough, snagged a trouser cuff on one of the iron pales but with a tug it was free, and once beyond the pales (as it's said).... The place was quiet, as one might expect. I paused and took a flask from my pocket, took a sip, just in case. I tried to make out the moving figure beyond the fence, beyond the fixed figures, the latter of which were, of course, abundant. The mist made a mess of depth of field, trying to gauge approximate distances. I started to move at a 45-degree angle from the fence, which should have sufficed. But once the fence was lost from view this became next to impossible. I neared a bench. Turning to sit, I came face to face with the cemetery dog. How long he'd been there, tailing me (minutes? years?), I'd no way of knowing. All the times you've felt breath on your neck, assumed a draft, and did not turn. Here boy, I said. Extended my hand. But he stayed put, a couple yards off. I pulled up my legs beneath me on the bench. Only the mist continued to move, in waves, veils, slow flocks of light. Birds began, which usually awakens me. Usually I'd shut the window at this time. Instead, I felt drowsy, I was in the prone position. Why I say "he." Why I say "boy." I've truly no idea what the dog's gender was.

Security located me just about dawn. Intact, untouched, the dog gone. After a

asthenia – weakness or loss of strength

asthma –

asyndesis – disorder of thought in which normal associations of idea are disrupted brief chat with the guard he took down my name but said they'd waive charges on the grounds my trespassing appeared to lack "intent." Suggested I not be found there again between the hours of dusk and dawn. Suggested I maybe have a chat with my doctor. I mentioned Bergman's *Hour of the Wolf*. He regretted not knowing it, knew only *Cries and Whispers*, *The Seventh Seal*, *The Passion of Anna*. We talked and talked. I was giddy with rapport, something, finding a common tongue. I would've been happy to stay there longer, but he had his report, the mists were lifting, the people blind with daylight were rising. I forgot to even mention the dog, to compliment them on the excellent training, until I was already halfway home. The streetcar slowed in the rush-hour traffic, I decided to why not stroll the remainder. It took a little over an hour and a half, by which time the mail had come, including (of course) your postcard from Nepal. Four weeks' time—I can hardly believe it! Under a month before we again— to just say we, to again be able! I checked my limbs for puncture wounds. How in the world can I feel this good? This week I start preparation for my fall course, "The Monster in Literature." I'm very excited. I shall make a categorical apology to Johnson. My shins in fact look cooked in milk. I need sun. Can it be that simple? It's nine in the evening and I've yet to have a drink. The bottle lurks, I know it's there, but I'm holding off. Holding off. 9:30 showing is

ataxia – shaky movements, unsteady gait due to brain's failure to regulate posture and direction of limbs

atony – state in which the muscles are floppy

atrophy – (even worse)

Murnau's *Nosferatu*. The first b-word of any application is "bacillemia," the presence of bacilli in the blood. Be that as it may, one persists. I think of the dams we built in Nepal, the bombs we escorted down upon Baghdad.

Here I sit with a garlic sandwich. You probably think I'm kidding. I am not kidding. The garlic, of all things, thrived this year. I will claw my way back to flesh and blood. I was human once. I'm certain.

authorization – (lack of)

autointoxication – poisoning by a toxin formed within the body

automobility – (lack of)

awe –

The Beautiful Children
by Michael Kenyon

We had breakfast at Norm's around three in the afternoon, bananas and candy bars. The bananas were green and the chocolate was melting. We were thinking, What a shock. We ate half the bananas and all the candy and talked about crossing the street. We talked about shoes. We felt good. Our shoes, what could you say about shoes? A wheelchair wheeled by the window, a beautiful cropped head loose as a balloon. The sky was dark blue and the sun hurt. We decided to have coffee. The place was full. We talked about what drives people, things like convenience, fear. We'd heard of this recluse who lived across town and wrote programs. We remembered eating whipped-up egg whites, sweet and baked over ice cream. There were donuts on one side of the table, coffee cups on the other. This was a sunny day in our lives. Sugar trailed from the donuts to the cups, sugar round the rims and slicks on the surfaces. We loved pastel sprinkles. We were tired because we'd been hunting day and night.

We clutched to our hearts small bags of fresh holes and got out on the street. We ate as we walked. We wondered how long it'd take to become a different person, how long teeth would last and could you invent yourself. We talked about filling in pitfalls. Some of us were bored or had pain from what, or lack of what, we couldn't remember, or didn't want to. We could cut out anything with a knife. We had reason to live. We looked through a window and saw a baby being fed. We imagined chasing leaves blowing across a field. We remembered forests, some of us, and strange paths between familiar places. We talked about the recluse across town. The programmer. We'd go there, go see him maybe. We told ourselves stories of decay and of things growing out of decay. It all played.

We talked about shoes. We were on a corner we liked and watching the shoes going by and comparing. We couldn't keep track. We went to the end of the block and back. We had to talk about shoes. Big jets were chasing across the sky and we couldn't hear ourselves but we had to talk about shoes anyway. We were saying, Eye holes, laces, soles, heels. We were saying, Who d'you think you are?

Nobody looked at us. We couldn't touch one another, only our own selves, that was true. We were saying, If you can't keep still, walk away.

We didn't want to help anyone. We made it so nothing changed, everything stayed the way we wanted. Pure. We clenched our teeth and talked about corruptions and total concepts.

We got back to shoes, haunted shoes. No one would pay attention. Shoes were too big or too small. We'd fall, maybe, and no one, not one of us, would check if that body still lived. It still played. Down there in the dark, under the cover we'd put over the pit. Shoes went on forever. We wondered when we'd turn into something. We couldn't stop there. If we ran no one would catch us. Some bodies were made to dance. We were skeletons with shoes. We were youth wasted on the young. We had fine little bellies. We were down at the heel. This was no place for children.

We sat on a bunch of crates and planks on buckets and some of us lay down and we passed the night sharing bottles and planning how to go about things, spending time on details. In the morning we saw stars crap out then sent someone to get information. We weren't staying where we were. If we decided to run, no one would catch us.

Nothing was wrong with us. We just couldn't feel anything. We had information people were hungry for, information about the universe. They didn't know. They hardly ever even tried.

We were walking down the block and one of us made a scoop shirt and we filled it with trash, butt ends, and grabbed handfuls and threw stuff at one another and bits of ash and leaf flew in our hair and we were laughing and choking, this dust so thick we couldn't see straight.

We played split with a knife. We combed out the dirt, combed and combed. We had to wait a while then, but not long. We were always waiting around. To have what we saw. Then we didn't want it. We were stoned and nothing ever changed but the color of the sprinkles. We collected what was left out. We had teeth that could bite through anything. We licked at sweetness, say sherbet, fudge, jam. We chewed garbage and lived. Our lips tingled. We were dangerous then. We walked down the aisles of a Superstore. We bit through what we stole and walked out empty. We bounced off cars and cracked windshields and lived. The invasion had begun. We were coming along the gully and we were savage.

We rolled down the hill and hit the wall of Norm's Donut Shop. We punched holes in the tires of cars parked in the alley. We went up the hill and skated down again. In Norm's we joked around. We waited for something to happen. Tow-truck drivers came in and gave us cigarettes. We talked about different things we'd eaten. Different ways we'd looked.

Jets in formation were flying overhead and we put hands over our ears. We had a big fight about whose hair was longest. We hustled out and raided the northside dumpsters. Down at the Gardens we were propositioned. We practiced jumping off picnic tables. Finch lay there and didn't move. We put the body by the No Exit sign and next day it was gone.

We ran the show. We were as sweet as candy on blue days. We knew we were being watched. We saw the gas prices were going up, coffee was going up. We lost Robin. We went to the Gardens and lay under the fountain. We talked about nothing but the winter. Our minds filled with dreams of glory. No milk, no sugar, but lots of chocolate. We caught a cat in a bag. We were ugly and wanted friends. Our straps kept slipping. The wind from the west smelled like something else. We said we'd always be together. We felt connected. We snapped off young shoots and saved them. Our weapons made sense, they shone, ratcheted, whirred. We let the cat go. We attended a traffic accident. Crow got stabbed and bled and recovered. It didn't matter what we did. We didn't know what we were doing and weren't responsible for anything. We wore striped and big-brimmed hats. We lived in alleys and spent time in the Gardens and at Norm's. We could never make cash machines work. We hunkered down in the rain. When it got too cold to sleep we went to the Emergency. We leaned against the glass and watched it get white. We talked and talked until we had nothing to say, then went to sleep.

We were affectionate and easy, slim and attractive. We were enterprising. We were lyrical and flexible and happy. We were rapt. We were humorous, honest, intelligent, natural. We were enchanting and bubbly. We were ambitious. We were romantic. We were shaggy, energetic, considerate, lean and strong. We were curious. We were semi-chunky, hot, dirty and sassy. We were muscular. We were adventurous. We were pathological. We were incarcerated.

We were changing. We didn't know what we meant.
    We went downtown to kick teeth. We had dinner at the soup kitchen. We used up all the toilet paper. People thought we were

cute. We thought we were cool. We stole all the time. We said, What is it good for? Good question. And threw it away. We felt happy.

We went in the pool with our clothes on. We were just swimming in the water and they were trying to get us out, poking us with sticks. We had to kiss this stone face just at the surface for good luck. We were swimming out of the way of the sticks. We got bruised in the end. We had to leave our shoes behind. We saw a baby crawling by and we all started howling like a baby, just howling and howling. This was later, on the boulevard, when we got dry, and it felt pretty good.

We were walking out of a cold night. We'd been out again all night. We were tired and bleeding from sores. A person saw us and took one of us back toward the sinking moon. We watched what was happening. We killed the person, fed the flesh to local pigs, and collected the bones in a bag which we buried in the Gardens.

We woke up screaming.

We had to keep warm.

For hours we passed houses with faces pressed against windows. Trees bent double in the wind. We were talking about the garden of bones. We told stories. "The Child Demands a Father." "The Two Fires." "The Dream of the Magic Birds." We moved to a new place between two buildings with warm walls, middle of the block, right across the street from the programmer, right across from the pawn shop and the TVs, right between two trees where birds slept. Moon rising through the branches. This was before the crack-up, everything frozen. Iced-over dumpsters. We stole sesame for the birds all winter. It seemed like we'd all promised to die, as if we all wanted to die. Some of us did. We wanted to die. We didn't know what to believe in or how to fight for it. We didn't want to live. We began to die. First our beauty died. We watched the birds fly up in the afternoons, earlier and earlier. Some days they didn't bother to fly out at all. They perched up there and fluffed their feathers and down below we worried about being left alone. We put our backs against the warm walls and felt cold to the bone and talked about how this would pass, the alley, the season, one another, the world, the universe. We closed our eyes. We said, Far out, the way the plains roll south into long valleys between tall mountains.

Cold broke us up. We didn't understand. We couldn't think straight. We were sensitive to cold. We weren't wearing enough clothes. We begged bus fare to the river and stood on the bridge and watched the water stop. We wanted to jump. We ran to get warm. It was getting late. We saw a pigeon with one leg hopping about inside the fence around a construction site. It was getting dark. The pigeon couldn't fly. We went out next morning to try to find the pigeon but it had gone. We'd made a mistake. We put our hands in our pockets and talked about birds, ships, trains, the moon, wild animals, storms. We were looking for weapons. We were on our way to a place we'd never been with a message for people we'd never met and the message would kill us or them. We played with knives and felt nervous. We played again and someone got hurt. No one wanted to be the pigeon.

In the Gardens they were digging up bones. We stood outside the ribbon and watched them shaking their heads. There were green shoots coming up in the alley. The river got going. Some of us disappeared. Some others arrived. We went to the Emergency when we needed something. We went to the airport when we got bored. We ran away when they chased us.

Nothing could stop us.

In summer we faded. Things seemed to roll about. Not us. The street. We were covered with travel dust. Buildings and people did a slight roll. We kicked a can. It rolled and shone. The street and the river and the alley all rolled up. Our eyes rolled. We made pig sounds. We got the shakes. We were unwashed and broken. We found a warehouse full of brown leather shoes with brass buckles. We recognized authority.

We relaxed. We put arms around one another's necks. Our ribs showed. We swam in the river, under the bridge. We were so hot. We stretched out in the water. We were nice and ready for the softness of one another. We were good buddies. We were dependable, durable, true blue. We looked up at everybody crossing the bridge and went under and pretended we were drowning and getting what we wanted. We almost seemed to have a life of our own. By night we were cool and rattled and jumpy. Our navels were deep. We could cut out anything with a knife, yet couldn't touch one another. We felt everything and it wasn't enough. People seemed breezy, asking for it. We wanted the feel of them. They looked cushiony and brushed and shiny. They looked like soft takes. We were shaking so hard we couldn't move. We had no heft, no substance, no finish. They were fluid. We hid. We were so light they blew us away. They were generous. They lived in color. Our brown shoes weren't enough. We made welts on their skin with our knives. We were in a sweat. We were anxious. We were invisible. We picked them up. They let us. We cut vents in their clothes. We were smoke. They didn't feel a thing. We eased into them. They were firm. We finished them off. They were surprised. For a second we were soft, gentle, lush. Almost delicate. And they were strong, with an edge. We looked through the torn cloth at the shape of the welts.

Thistleheads exploded in the alley and we couldn't stop sneezing. We held our futures. Nights were short. Our faces were ugly and familiar and all wrong.

We held our shit for days, then held our piss for hours, and drank a lot of coffee. It was full moon. We went out to the golf course and couched around one of the holes. Everything was blue. The sky came at us. We'd never felt so empty. We talked about climbing onto roofs and lifting tiles and reaching into houses and ripping out wires and starting the big fire. We talked about digging a deep long tunnel where we could live underground. We talked about stealing a train and filling a coach with dirt and having a garden with fruit trees. We talked about knife fights in arenas in front of big crowds. We wanted to be caught and held. We wanted to die. We wanted to tear out throats. We wanted to hide away. We loved the people around us and wanted to attract their attention. We wanted to kill them and drink their blood and become them. We wanted to protect them. We wanted the skin of our bodies, the skin of our bodies, the skin of our bodies. We said, If you think you are, you're not. We said, If you think you do, you don't. We said, It doesn't work backwards. We are the same person. We said, This is now.

We hunted.

We were looking for the end of the gully. The gully was an alley in the gut. An opening in the skin. Knives would cut through. We wanted what was on the other side. True heart. We called bullet holes false navels. We counted the generations. We got lost in how many it had taken to make us. We got lost in the stars. The lights went out. We counted so many we got dizzy. We said the buck stops here. We said we didn't feel a thing. We said it's crazy up here, back in time, deeper and deeper, fewer and fewer, more and more.

In the alley green ferns broke the dirt we thought was cement. We thought, What a shock.

We went into the Emergency with our hats on backward. We took turns in the wheelchairs. We waited in the waiting room and watched TV. People were crying on the phone. We booted the vending machines and got stuff we didn't like. The donuts were stale. Security threw us out. We watched the rain. We stood in the bus shelter and watched the rain. Ambulances kept arriving and unloading. They kept mopping up the blood.

We had blades. We wanted to stay in the dark and play with the switches. We wanted to get caught and escape. We made bombs out of pipes and fireworks and bottles and gas and rags. We hid everything and collected more. At night we ran and ran. We were conspicuous and crazy and mumbled so no one knew what we meant. Jets were chasing across the sky. We closed our eyes and waited. We kept on talking, running in the dark, playing. We had nothing but plans. The worst winter. The best chocolate éclairs. We went to a zoo and ate ice cream. We had a fever and slept for a week. We got sick and died. We chewed pills and got pierced. We were a freak show. A TV crew followed us around.

They asked us all kinds of questions. We told them what had happened to us, the truth. The sky came at us in waves. We'd never felt so good. They asked did we know what country we were in. We gave them some information, a taste. They asked what country we'd like to be in. We gave them all our information, opened ourselves up. We waited to see what they'd do. What they'd offer of themselves in return. We had nothing left except this wait and it didn't last long. They said we'd fallen through the cracks. We were lost. We were losers. We were victims, the final victims. They told us what country we were in. We showed our bellies. We showed our blades.

They showed us the movie and we couldn't believe how cool we were. Savages. It all played. Unbelievable, the way we moved. Our eyes shone. What could this world offer us? We'd been sold down the river and forgotten. We'd run away and ruined ourselves. We'd inherited a generation's loneliness. We were heroes. We were stars. In the movie our faces were dirty. At the end, the sun went down and we shuffled around in the dust of the alley. Colored bits of light made a line across the screen and music started to play. We looked small. Brave. Everlasting.

We torched Norm's and visited the suburbs.

Church bells were ringing. The weather turned cold. Everything got quiet. Anything that happened, happened in front of us instead of down the block, across the street.

We felt uneasy. We had to do something. Nobody was home. Things kept going off by themselves. Alarms, sprinklers, lights, doors. What we had to do was get back downtown. This time, time was waiting, not us. There were no stores. The lawns were empty and green. We whispered about what there was to talk about. We broke some windows, took a couple of things we didn't recognize. We'd made a mistake. We couldn't find the church. We couldn't find a bus. There were no blocks. Streets went in circles. We tossed the stuff we'd taken. We felt stupid. Everything looked the same.

We found a shopping mall. People were going in, coming out. We talked to them. They gave us money. We used the phone. We talked to the operators. We went inside and looked at birds and fish and animals in tanks and cages. We pretended to listen to people playing music. We put the money in a hat. We were afraid. For the first time, we were afraid. We looked for a dark corner. There was a crowd by one door. We hung around and looked at earrings and teeth. We were last in line, for what we didn't know. We greeted one another like old friends. We said, How's tricks. When we saw someone we wanted we looked the other way. We had side vision. We had bodies and felt dizzy. We didn't look at what we wanted. We didn't want anything. We didn't want to go in. We didn't want to stay. We didn't want to go on. Everyone was staring at us.

We looked out of the glass doors at cars parked between the painted lines. The road out of there was long and straight. We talked till all we could hear was wind. All we could hear was wind. Everyone here was our enemy. The road was long and straight and lonely. A piece of garbage blew down the middle. We didn't like any of it. What we'd do was stick out our thumbs and show our bellies. We'd get a ride. We'd get a ride.

A Thin White Hand
by Kenneth J. Emberly

We had been drinking that night, as usual, and I was feeling very tired. The rooming house was quiet, and I was expecting old Schulte to fall asleep any minute. He was clearly worn out. But suddenly he began speaking again, only this time his words were not slurred, and although he was staring into space, his eyes did not have that customary vacant glassy look. His voice was calm, almost dull, yet he seemed agitated somehow, as if he were unburdening himself without feeling the slightest sense of relief. I listened, convinced for once that what I was hearing might very well be true. And if it were true in any way I would never again be able to view Schulte as merely a tiresome old drunkard, sometimes pathetic, sometimes aggravating, but essentially harmless to everyone but himself.

Usually I didn't credit Schulte's talk with a whole lot of truth. When drunk, he was morose, and rambling, and sick. When sober, he was bitter, and edgy, and given to making absurd speeches about anything that crossed his path or went through his addled mind. Often, the only difference between drunk and sober was the degree of vehemence with which he expressed his confused notions and tangled reminiscences. Like a preacher shouting down the doubts of a backsliding congregation, Schulte would twist things this way and that so they'd fit the particular mold of his story. Concern for the truth rarely entered into it. Hunched over the rickety card-table in that dismal common room off the hall, his dirty gray hair falling forward over his emaciated face, he'd start out telling a story about his travels, and then suddenly, without warning, the whole thing would shift and he might launch into another story about jail, or about the high life he'd supposedly led (and which had landed him behind bars, he said, too many times for counting). You could believe what you wanted to. He never paid much mind to a listener's reaction. And when he was done he would be dead drunk and passed out in his chair.

I had spent the entire miserable winter cooped up in that west side rooming house listening to Schulte, and sometimes I'd watch him sleeping, his breath catching in drawn-out drunken rattles, and I'd mull over what he'd spoken. I'd try to sort out the truth from the lies. Or sometimes I'd just settle back and let the whole strange reality of his tale come over me, like a dream. But on that one particular occasion he went beyond mere storytelling. He made what amounted to a confession.

His flat matter-of-fact tone and scrupulous attention to detail were striking, as he related events that had allegedly taken place in the countryside not far from the city in which we lived. He described the area in minute detail—the roads, the landmarks, the distances between farms and so on—though it had all happened many years ago, relating the story with unnerving detachment, the way a person suddenly awakened from a sound sleep might relate a dream he had just been having. I was fascinated, and the longer he went on, the more I could see it, as if it were my own dream, or my own memory, and a horrific one at that.

When he had finished I watched him sink into a restless drunken sleep, his bony hands on the table, fingers splayed, his head drooping down on his sunken chest. And his story, or confession, or nightmare, kept going around and around in my head, until I knew that I'd never get any rest until I went to the place he had described and saw it for myself.

Shortly before dawn I left him there and went out to my car, a beat-up white Datsun, which was about the only thing of value I owned at the time. I was agitated and feeling sick, though strangely lucid, the way you do after a night of drinking, but I was also excited by the knowledge, or suspicion, that just thirty or forty miles away there was a place—the Watson farm, he'd called it—that I felt I knew as intimately as if I'd lived there, though I'd never seen it.

I drove through the city in something of a daze, heading west, and then south, breaking into open farm country, bleak and frozen at that time of year, the dairy pastures and cornfields just white and empty. And as I drove deeper into the stark winter country, I remembered everything Schulte had told me. How a young girl had found him hiding in the stable and, without a word exchanged between them, brought him food, how she did this at dawn, leaving it outside the door, how she concealed him from her whole family, how she kept him like another animal on the farm—captive, and hungry, and fascinating—how their secret was never uncovered, how the stable remained in darkness, ruined, rotting, inviolate, how a young girl found him. I remembered it word for word, following the roads and passing the places he had named.

There was a light layer of snow and ice on the ground, otherwise I'd never have ventured down the farm's rutted laneway, for fear of getting stuck. I left the car when I came to an old bridge over a creek. It had taken me far enough. I could see the ruined farm buildings on top of the hill: the square, three-story red-brick house, with its empty, black windows, and the collapsed barn, one end of the roof nearly touching the frozen ground, like an animal knocked to its knees, and not far off, but seeming isolated somehow, the old stable, long and narrow, and looking ready to give way at the least gust of wind. There was not another house or building within sight. The farm was isolated by a low range of hills to the west, and the winding gravel road by which I had come was now cut off from view by a dense stand of pines that followed the course of the creek. It looked exactly as Schulte had described it, at least in terms of its layout, for when he had last been here it had been a thriving, reasonably prosperous farm, not a deserted ruin.

For a while I simply stood there, wondering if I would feel compelled to go any closer. I closed my eyes and thought that if I remembered everything he had said it might be enough. I would see the bridge over the creek, the ruined buildings, the light snow on the bare waxy ground, and then I would look away, turn around, flee. Or I would advance cautiously over the bridge, listening for the piercing whine of wood splitting underfoot, and then, when I was safely on the other side, I would pause and stare up at the house, my mind free of any longing to fill the place with ghostly inhabitants, free of any interest in the dilapidated barn and derelict stable, and when I felt the cold numbing my feet I would turn around and leave, having seen enough.

Treeless barren ground surrounded the buildings on the low hill, and across the rolling landscape the fence posts marked irregular snowy fields. To the house, then, and its dry and empty rooms, so still and frosted, the wallpaper hanging in brittle strips, the floorboards unsafe for walking, the door hinges that screamed at a touch. On the threshold, a darkened staircase leading to the blackness of the second floor, and to the right of the stairs a closed door, its white paint flaking, the transom shattered. Not venturing down the hallway, not approaching the closed door, not mounting the darkened stairs, listening, hearing nothing, or hearing the faintest rustle perhaps, like dry leaves or a stiff skirt brushing the wall, like fingertips on the paper, there, on the other side of the closed door, in the blackness at the top of the stairs, at the far end of the narrow hall, receding in silence.

The light was very poor, but I could make out the pattern on the peeling wallpaper, small bunches of flowers tied with ribbon, and some pale squares where pictures had hung. Very clearly now: tiny round flowers on slender stems, tied like sheaves of wheat, on every visible wall, not only downstairs, but leading to the second floor as well, and doubtless beyond that.

Knowing that her small room was on the top floor at the very back of the house, he would watch for her. He told me that he pressed his face to the wall of the stable, peering through gaps in the warped boards. He would wait, sometimes for long hours, hoping to see her at the window, or to see a light. How he stood there trembling, how he felt the splinters of those boards against his cheeks, how he fought the hunger in his belly and the fear that she would expose him, or forget him, deny his existence completely and never leave the solid red-brick house again, and knowing that her room was at the top of those stairs, I could imagine it all.

I thought that if I imagined this perfectly, subservient to the recollection of his words, I would back through the open door, bury my face in the collar of my coat, and quickly walk away from that sad emptiness. I would hear my feet plodding through the fragile gloss of snow and I would not look back. Or I would place my foot on the bottom step of that staircase, and I would hear the wood groan, feel the railing under my hand (not thinking of the girl's hand in the same place, not thinking of the girl's foot on the same step, feeling nothing of her presence or any other presence) and, judging the stairs unsafe, I would back away and retreat outside. I would deny any further interest in these frigid ruinous buildings. They had been stripped clean, and the only thing left was what could be imagined, or what could be faithfully recollected in detail, as one remembers the dead. And, as one leaves the dead in peace, so, too, would I leave this place.

He told me that he had spent several days studying the farm from a distance, noting the absence of a dog on the property, observing how no one bothered to go near the abandoned stable, which he could plainly see was already a ruin that no one had bothered to tear down. And the more he watched the stable, the more it took on the appearance of a refuge. Even with its sagging walls and holes in the roof it seemed as safe and inviolable as a convent, and one night he slipped down out of the hills and buried himself in the rotting hay of a stall where no horse (nor any other creature) had been for a very long time. The well-lighted house and barn seemed as far away as a distant country and he slept soundly at last.

A THIN WHITE HAND

He was awakened at dawn by noise from the barn, and for a while he observed the farmer's activities from behind the stable walls. Then he slept again, troubled by hunger and fear, and when he next awoke he caught a fleeting glimpse of a young girl observing him from the stable door. Afterward, he waited for them to come, to chase him back into the hills. But they never came. He remembered the girl, the same girl he had observed countless times from his hiding place near the farm. A strange girl, she never participated in the daily round of the farm, but simply wandered from place to place, a solitary child, withdrawn and likely simple-minded. She did not tell anyone about the fugitive in the abandoned stable, so no one came to chase him away, no one knew he was there.

At dawn the next day she returned with food. Thin and silent, and not at all wary, she behaved in a calm, matter-of-fact way, as if he were merely some new animal that required feeding. She made no effort to see him or to talk to him, and she never came near the stable except at dawn.

How she came every day, how he would wait, how his stomach would first freeze and then dance, when he finally saw her slipping away from the house bearing bread or fruit, or perhaps leavings from the previous night's table, some simple food wrapped in paper, how he heard her coming and crouched ready by the hole in the closed door of the stable, and then how she dropped the paper, pausing, her white feet visible as she waited for his hand to reach out, and then how her white feet padded softly across the bare ground as she returned to the house, how the sick fevered cats crowded close around his ankles, mewling, hissing, staggering and gaunt, how he told me to imagine the dark, and the waiting, and the greasy paper torn to shreds by the cats, and knowing that her room was at the top of those stairs, I imagined it all.

Surprised that the steps did not groan, I continued up the stairs, gripping the railing so tightly that my sweaty palms shrieked on the wood every time I moved my hand. It was dark on the second-floor landing. All the doors were closed, and as I moved in a spiral toward the next flight of stairs I counted them—four white doors that would open into separate high-ceilinged bedrooms. I knew that if I opened those four doors I would see everything exactly as he had described it: the plain white walls, the wide pine floorboards, the heavy ceiling fixtures, the recessed window frames, the view over the frozen countryside, every room cold, and still, and eaten with decay. His description would prove to be accurate, because his description of everything else—from the front hall and staircase to the pattern on the wallpaper—had been accurate. I no longer had any doubts. I moved, instead, toward the weak blue light emanating from the third floor. I moved slowly but with less caution, trusting that this last flight of stairs would hold me as they had once held the girl.

Upright, on its hind legs, the cat had danced toward him. His boot caught it under the chin and sent the animal backward across the stone floor. But within seconds it had recovered, and it came at him again, emitting a low rolling growl that heightened to a sudden scream the closer it got, ears flattened against its skeletal head, claws extended, every muscle in its emaciated body twitching as it prepared to spring. He looked quickly for something with which to strike it—a board, a stick, a rock—but there was nothing at hand. And then from the corner of his eye he saw it leap, saw its narrow gray body lengthen, airborne, screaming. As his arms instinctively went up over his face and he lurched to one side, he was certain that he could feel the claws sinking into his flesh. But he was wrong. In the dim light he saw that the cat had simply fallen back to the floor and, instead of the mindless fury it had displayed only seconds before, it now wavered unsteadily on its four paws, head drooping, racked once more by the sickness that had driven it mad. No longer bristling with rage, it seemed scrawny, fragile, incapable of defending itself, let alone attacking a creature many times its size. But this sudden incapacitation, he realized, would only be temporary.

Before long it would shake off this strange spell of weakness and become maddened with fury again. Searching more calmly now, he soon found a length of board nearby. The diseased cat was staggering, almost crawling, in a wide erratic circle. It seemed totally unaware of its surroundings. When he jabbed its hind legs it simply fell over, breathing heavily, and then rose unsteadily once again. He tried to make it change direction by prodding it with the board, but although the pain caused it to hesitate and waver a few times, it always recovered and continued to drag itself in a circle. He raised the board high above his head and then brought it down on the cat's skull. He did this several times until there was nothing left of the animal's head but a bloody pulp of fur, and bone, and jelly.

There was a window at the top of the stairs, a small square window of blue stained glass set high in the wall. I thought that if I remembered that vague blue light I would see myself backing down the stairs. Or I would call out. I would shout. I would scream. And then with silence returning, I would feel the stairs giving way beneath me, snapping like dry sticks, as I spun around looking for something to grab onto. To the top of the stairs, then, and the little hallway suffused with blue, the dark water stains on the wallpaper, the open door at the end of the hall. Not expecting any reply to my shout, not even listening for one, or hearing the faintest laugh perhaps, like the stifled glee of a child in hiding, like the irrepressible giggle that precedes the springing of a trap, deepening to a malevolent hate-filled snarl, abruptly silenced, I could imagine him killing the cat in vivid detail: how he crushed its skull, how he took it to the hole in the stable door and shoved it through for the girl to take away, how he hunted the other cats, one by one.

He was certain that she wouldn't care what happened to the cats. They were just wild creatures, he said, waiting to die from one sickness or another, and he had never seen her take the slightest interest in the animals around the farm. So, when she left him food the next morning and took the dead cat away with her, he figured the whole thing was over and done with. But he must have been wrong, because the day after that the girl didn't show up. He waited hungry by that hole in the door, straining his ears to hear her feet padding the ground, but she never came. And the next morning it was the same. He was half crazy with hunger, and the only thing he had to satisfy his belly was water from the old pump at the back of the stable. Finally, on the third day, she returned. He crawled over, desperate for whatever food she might drop, but when he saw what she'd left he was sick. It looked like rotten potato peelings, or something worse. He tried to eat it, but he couldn't keep it down. All that day he watched her moving around inside the house, and in the evening he saw the light go on in her room, and he watched that window until the light went out, until the whole farm was pitch dark and there was nothing to be seen on a moonless night.

The next day she came with the same inedible mess, only this time she stood outside waiting to see what he'd do. When he didn't reach out to take it she went away. He was truly sick by now and feeling very weak, but when he heard her return soon after he roused himself and waited to see what would happen next. It was then that he felt fear like he'd never felt before, he said, because the girl was walking around the stable pouring gas from a can. He could smell it. He could hear it splashing against the walls. If she lit a match the whole stable would go up in flames. But she didn't light a match. She just went back to the place where the food lay and waited. He could scarcely breathe, waiting for the fire, but suddenly he understood and he reached out for the food. Only then did she leave.

At the end of the narrow hall, at her open door hanging loose on its rusted hinges, I could see where the black iron latch had been snapped off, splintering the dry blond wood. And in the door itself there were three long vertical cracks, or fractures, as if the door had withstood a severe battering, as if the wood had strained and then cracked before the latch gave way and the door flew open into that small square room.

From now on, he said, he ate whatever she left for him in the morning, snatching it greedily the minute it hit the ground. Some mornings it was real food. Other days she'd leave him things not fit for man or animal to eat. But he took it, just the same. He could tell that she was enjoying the whole thing. She was too young to know what real hunger was like, too simple to know that power over another living creature, no matter how fragile, was a dangerous thing. It must have seemed like a game to her. But he remembered the smell of that gasoline, and that was no game, not to him.

How he ate the food, hoarding his strength, keeping still, how he watched her pacing in the yard, just like an animal herself, long-limbed, quick, and solitary, how he watched her taut young body, light and easy, like a young animal coming to its own, a wild creature surrounded, protected by her family, those lumbering burdened people who walked with the same measured steps, the same sloping shoulders, no matter where they went, no matter why, glancing every now and again at the coltish stranger in their midst, sometimes reproaching her, sometimes coaxing her, but ultimately leaving her to herself (and to him who was watching her, too, without them knowing it, watching her in a different way) and standing in the doorway of her room I could imagine it all.

Her room was narrow, wide enough for a bed and a dresser, with little space between. I noticed immediately that the wallpaper in her room bore a different design from that found in the rest of the house. Instead of bunches of flowers uniformly tied like sheaves of wheat, here the pattern was of spring bouquets, delicate and bright, arranged loosely. I could stand in the doorway and see across that short space to the window in the end wall, the window that looked out on the yard, and the stable, and beyond to the snowy white fields.

Now he took to leaving the stable at night, he said, though freedom wasn't what he really wanted. Freedom meant that you might get caught, so you had to give it to yourself in small measured doses. That way it wouldn't go to your head and make you reckless. He had learned, he said. He knew how to wait until the fear of capture and the memory of imprisonment had died down, and walking around in the broad daylight didn't put his heart somewhere up in his throat. So he slipped out of the stable a little bit at a time. He scoured the periphery of the farm, avoiding the barn so as not to make the animals restless, going out only when the ground was firm so as not to leave footprints, touching nothing he couldn't put back as he'd found it. And in the morning, he said, neither the girl nor anyone else could tell that he'd been out—staring in their windows, creeping around their doors, watching their house like a hunter watching his prey, and them sleeping all the while.

How he watched the light go on in her room each morning, how he waited behind the door, listening for her footsteps, the soft tread of a pale white simpleton coming down to feed her beast in the stable, how in his mind he was already far down the road, far away in some other barn or stable, or scrounging around in a vast anonymous city, how those last days and nights there in the stable were like a dream, the outcome of which he already knew, how he understood that it would just be a matter of him getting up some night and walking through the dream from beginning to end, of settling an account and moving on, and looking down from her window I could see it happening.

I could see how he moved across the yard, slow and deliberate in the moonlight, how he went to the shed and then around to the back door, knowing that it would be unlocked. In the kitchen he paused and let his eyes adjust to the increased darkness of the interior. He gave himself time to get a feel for the house, its strange smell, its warmth, the sharp corners of its smooth papered walls. And then he moved across the floor, mindful of its creaking, the edges of carpets, the legs of tables. In the front hall he felt for the wooden banister railing, and then slowly, very gently, he began to climb the stairs. He could hear a big clock ticking somewhere and the occasional groan of the old house settling in the night. On the second-floor landing he paused to let his heart stop pounding. There were four white doors, all closed, and the only light came from the moon shining through a small blue stained-glass window at the top of the next flight of stairs. But he could see well enough. And when he had passed through those doors and entered the square high-ceilinged rooms, he could see quite clearly, for the curtains were open. He could see the clothes thrown across chairs, and the small framed pictures on dressers, and the tiny handles of drawers and cabinets, above which there were mirrors, each one reflecting the scene with sharp glassy clarity: the solid wooden footboards, the sleeping figures stretched out full-length or curled up tight beneath the sheets, the dark heads exposed on pillows, and then an arm protectively thrown over a face too late, a bare white foot kicking out at nothing, a pale hand raised, clawing the air, then sinking down, quivering, going still.

And with every door opened now, the hallway was flooded with hard white moonlight. He could see every post of the banister, and every flower on the wallpaper, and every step up to that third floor. And up to that point the dream had unfolded smoothly, efficiently, and according to plan. But now he heard himself shouting—not words, but sounds—smashing the stillness like a bone, like a skull, shattering the dream out of some strange uncontrollable perversity.

When he heard the girl open her door, he started climbing that last flight of stairs, moving fast because the dream was gone. He saw her frozen in the doorway, small and blue in her loose white shift, and then the door was shut. She was hidden behind a barrier of frail white wood, trapped and waiting. He smashed his way in. It was not difficult. But the room was empty. He saw the window open and ran to it. There, on the ground three floors below, lay a white form. Her arms and legs bent at odd angles, the girl lay sprawled face down on the bare earth. Her head was twisted toward her right shoulder at such an acute angle that he had no doubt her neck was broken.

For a long time he just stayed there leaning from her window, breathing the night air, letting quiet return, staring down at his broken quarry. Finally he went down to drag her off, stopping briefly on the second landing to close the four white doors.

But when he reached the spot where she had fallen he found nothing there. It was impossible. He had seen her. The fall had broken her neck. Yet she was gone. Panic-stricken, he ran from place to place all over the farm, searching for her, sometimes stealthy, sometimes wild, shouting, crashing through the house from top to bottom, scouring the barn, the stable, the bare earth itself. But he could not find her. Many times he thought maybe he had caught a glimpse of her slipping away in her loose white shift, but when he went in pursuit he found nothing, not even a trace. And there were so many places she could hide: buildings, basements, lofts, the tall grass, the stalls of nervous animals, around corners, behind rocks, behind doors, under beds, in closets. Yet he searched them all and turned up nothing. Thinking she might have made a run for the distant road, he raced down the laneway, knowing that she could easily have ducked into the trees anywhere along the way. He was frantic.

By dawn, though, his panic had given way to exhaustion. Whether it was that exhaustion or some intuitive sense that caused him to override reason, he was somehow convinced that she had never actually left the farm. Worse, he had the growing suspicion that she was not so much hiding as waiting, biding her time somewhere, calm and watchful. He wanted to deny such things. But he could not. Everywhere he walked, every place he paused to look around, he had the feeling that she was there, too, not with him, but nearby. And the sounds—the animals growing restless, neglected in the dawn, the birds breaking into piercing calls, the long grass stirring in the first morning breeze—all served to further confuse his senses, so that at times he thought he heard her laughing, and at others, crying, and he began to wander aimlessly now, staggering from building to building without plan or purpose. If he closed his eyes he was immediately back in the night, leaning from her window, staring at her on the ground, seeing her there cleanly and clearly by moonlight, her neck broken. And when he opened his eyes, was that a thin white arm disappearing around a door frame, a body stepping back into darkness, moving through the long grass, sliding out of sight? There was madness gaining on him like fever on a sick man.

For how long he wandered on that farm, and through what nightmares of mind, he could not say. And how he left there, what he took with him, he did not know. But he did leave without finding her, though she was there somewhere, she had to be. Of that, at least, he was certain.

How he traveled, lying low, keeping still, circling the countryside like a bird of prey demented with hunger, not daring to go back, never able to stay far away, how at last he sank toward the city, to a street, to a house, to a room, how he stared at the night, like a man waiting to finish a dream, haunted and tormented by its elusiveness, by never knowing how it will end, certain only that it will, because all dreams do, even the worst. And standing there at her window, touched once by a breeze as soft and cool as a thin white hand, I could imagine it all, as if she were there, and it was all possible, it was all true.

The Apostle
by Madeline Sonik

Senga allowed the snake to uncoil like a gold chain around her belly. For a moment, she heard the eternal silence of death, saw its open, brown mouth, its black, greedy molars worn to nubs, and felt its arrow-sharp tongue. Her naked feet found the drum rhythms surely, as acknowledged wives find slippers in darkness. Her body connecting, her bones fluid fire.

Men paid money to see her dance. They sat at the edges of cabriolet chairs and teetered like divers. Some threw paper money and gold coins that bounced like bells off the thick, glass walls of her vivarium. But once swallowed in death's black throat, Senga saw and heard nothing. It was only the pulse that touched her. Only the breath of the snake.

Other dancers veiled themselves in her shadow. It was the rancid butter she applied to calm the snake, they said, that kept her flesh so young. She came from far away, danced for many years, mothered several children whom she abandoned. But to choose a venomous cobra instead of a young, harmless python? That was a mystery none could explain or understand. Even Nick, the owner of The Viper's Pit, who needed an industrial broom to sweep up the gratuities after Senga's performances, couldn't understand. He'd had his lawyers draw up a document releasing him from liability, and Senga agreed to sign. He took a sizable cut of the money thrown by the crowd, and knew no other dancer who could pack the club and make him rich as she could; still he would have paid a tidy amount himself to anyone who could tell him why she did it.

Embraced by the snake, Senga's body moved like elastic. Ankles, thighs, belly, midriff, breasts, encircled clockwise, counterclockwise, in patterns of infinity. She. Her golden hooded partner. Twin flames, erect then melding. Naked limbs braiding to snake. Tongue whispering to snake; snake woven human. It burned the eyes of men, of jealous dancers, who called her crazy and would have done almost anything to take her place. It left a taste in the mind of something savored and forgotten. A lost memory that can find no expression.

"Wasn't that something she did with that snake?" the men muttered to each other, to Nick, to the foam of their beer. "Whatyacallit?" The image already faded. And so they would have to come again, see again, burn again, forget again.

No dancer would ever follow Senga, no matter what the terms. There was an unstated code at The Viper's Pit, an unspoken hierarchy, with Senga always the last-to-dance queen.

After her performance, people staggered home, chairs turned on table tops, Nick counted money. Senga dressed in the bare, gray light of a small changing room, then stroked her blunt-nosed partner, enjoying the ricey texture of his still warm skin before placing him into a round wicker carrier.

The streets outside still glowed with flashing neon, rain puddles sparkled like road stars. Senga, now mortal in flat rubber boots, carried home her treasure, humming gently, feeling his tired weight in her fingers, making her way past the junkies, the crack houses, the two overworked prostitutes at the corner who pushed hair out of each other's eyes, and the dark maroon car that slowed to pick them up. She followed the winding alley paths in darkness, feeling sound vibrate on her lips and the steady powerful wind pushing at her back. It contained the strength of her grandmother, the strength of her grandmother's grandmother, and a voice bent low to embrace both her and her partner, to cradle them in a kind of feathery hammock.

There had been a time when Senga could not hear the voice, when she could not remember the first woman who loved her. A time when as a small, skinny child, a refugee, her mind had been wiped clean by angels, her grandmother's voice made foreign.

Yet even before she understood, the voice held her in darkness when the world disappeared; when the woman who was her mother saw dark reflections with her bright, glacial eyes, the voice wrapped her tightly in a sweet, mossy blanket of olive and kept her warm.

And then, she touched the snake. Its bright body sidewinding in dusty clay, its shining, ball-bearing eyes knowing and playful. She touched its small, lithe head, felt her finger become its concertina, its delicate whipping tongue lash and finally glide through her.

She was only a child, but recalls how the sky ripped open and the sun turned black, falling like a smoldering apple to the earth. How she lay suspended and paralyzed in the center of a hurricane, her grandmother rocking at her side in a chair fashioned from oak bows, stroking snake skin, words tumbling from her wrinkled mouth like meteors, until her language was known.

"Come sit on my lap, child." The words penetrated her like a thousand tiny fangs. They shot lightning into her veins.

"You hear me now, don't you?"

She could not move, but felt her body gathered up, like water absorbed in a cloud. The fluorescent hospital lights and acrid oxygen did not welcome her. A smiling nurse patted her hand, and the thin, white, scented woman who was her mother repeated, "Praise God, it's a miracle."

Plastic tubes whorled and twisted from the child's body like strings on a marionette, and her weak hands made gestures to remove them.

"No!" they told her, tying her ridiculously small body to the bed, taping her fingers together, securing her wrists to the metal bed frame with coarse towels.

Her throat seethed, it was as if every nerve had been scraped naked, as if every fiber of her body had become a conduit for unendurable pain. She longed only to be back where she had been, feeling the caress of the old woman's words.

"You're a wildcat," some doctor told her, "a real fighter."

She writhed and thrashed about, and the woman who was her mother half closed her pale, imploring eyes, and a nurse with a sharp silver stinger delivered liquid sleep.

The child's eyes, fierce and brown with pupils as large as moons, felt the world dissolve. Faces broke apart like puzzle pieces, words spun out of control over vast expanses of time. And the old woman, honey-colored, knobbly-elbowed, with teeth as wide and gapped as canyons, took the child onto her strong rocking lap, into her secret center.

There, in her folds, stories and songs traveled like molten spirit. "It was a long, long, long time ago, child," her grandmother hummed, "such a long time ago, everyone wants to forget."

But the child did not forget. The child would not forget. She would stretch her small bones wide open and drink the deep, sticky nectar of the past. She would feed upon it with a hunger that had crawled and gnawed within her before she'd known life. And when finally returned to the unseemly stagnant world, to the hollow tin voices and stainless steel reflections, she would hold it all within her like a precious secret. Hold it there, in her own private darkness.

If anything could be done for the child, the doctor could not say what. Test after test showed nothing organically wrong. Physically, she had made a miraculous recovery. But afterward, there were frighteningly long periods of silence, then days and days when the child would babble incoherently and, finally, seizures.

The woman who was her mother locked the child in the hall closet, her hands trembling as she turned the key. At times she thought it was Satan who had come upon the child. Satan in the guise of a snake, just as he had arrived in the garden of Eden, and she begged the minister of her church to intervene.

But the minister prided himself in being level-headed. It could not be Satan, he told the woman. "Why should Satan strike your child? You? When there are so many others to take who don't have recourse to God?"

The child was examined by neurological specialists, seen by psychiatrists. She was asked to play in sandboxes with little plastic toys, draw pictures with bright magic markers, recite dreams, but it was always the snake: the snake, as big as the biggest buildings; the ghost snake no one but she saw; the snake who slept under her pillow, hid between the walls of her house; the snake who lived everywhere.

The seizures worsened and could not be predicted. The child could not go to school like an ordinary child. She could not do simple things.

Sometimes she stood in the center of the small, treeless fenced yard hissing until the woman who was her mother had to drag her away. It was humiliating, terrifying, debasing, yet the woman knew she could not blame the child.

And then the woman was told about a special place, a special school, where the child would be kept clean and fed. And on holidays, the woman could visit. She could bring boxes of chocolates, birthday cakes, and sweaters; she could go there first, before she made any decisions, inspect the grounds, see for herself the beautiful gardens, speak to the staff.

Here, the child fell most deeply into the folds of her grandmother's skirt. Days and nights of induced sleep converged and no words hindered.

"They want you to forget, child," her grandmother rasped, "just like they all, but baby child, you hang on."

She wrapped the child in an old, clear, snake skin, the outline of folds and milky, triangular scales obscuring vision. With a long claw needle she sutured.

"This'll keep 'em out," she hummed, "this ole skin'll keep you safe till you ready to bust free."

And for years the child became invisible, strapped to a hollow metal bed frame in the institution, eyes unblinking, as her soul traveled in the grandmother's world.

It was the grandmother who named her Senga, the grandmother who taught her to dance with snakes.

"You gotta make the connection right, honey. Feel the roots of your feet. Dig 'em in deep enough, so nothin' can move you." The snake skulls strung around the old woman's neck shook and grinned. Fire flared in their empty sockets. "You got it, baby. You got the gift."

Contained in the warmth of the grandmother's world, Senga learned to see and listen. The palms of her hands tingled with the smallest movements, her breath absorbed images, her flesh heard. She learned to trust the snakes. To let them roam her body, explore her mind, fill her with their golden, wild fire.

"Everyone's wantin' to forget where they come from," the old woman murmured. "Everyone likes to pretend there ain't no startin' place. But you, honey, you gonna take that gift back and remind 'em in time."

So Senga danced like a fuse. She danced like a beacon. Her body substanceless, light, able to shine and cast shadow, able to bring vision as well as blind. She danced and experienced her self becoming, her child body stretching, filling with wakefulness, the flare of her brilliance, the heat of her kinesis, setting the world ablaze.

It was thought to have begun in an antiquated boiler room in the basement. Hundreds perished trying to escape. But Senga slid from the sleep of her grandmother's world, crawled across the melting tile floor of the institution, slithered through voracious flames. Her skin smoking and smoldering, steaming like volcanic pools.

The steely door was not bolted in the wing where her bed blistered, where sightless women and voiceless girls writhed in the ashes of their own flesh. The back draft scoured the walls clean of paint, licked innards out, scattered charred teeth like dice, until the hazy, guiltless morning when the fire was extinguished.

Few bodies were recovered. Most disappeared as completely as if they had never existed. The child was thought to be among them, but Senga had made her escape. She crawled out into the surrounding parkland and covered herself with the healing chill of earth. She slept beneath a large, gray oak, its empty twining branches providing shelter. And when she woke, she knew she glistened. The old skin of the grandmother lay heaped at her naked feet like waves of dusty moss.

She would not go back to the grandmother's world now, but would receive messages like a cadence of leaves caught in an arc of restless wind. There were things to be had on the slick, black streets: food and clothing, silver needles, sex, and money. Even the cobra she found there. He had been smuggled from another country as a conversation piece, used to kill a junkie who could not pay what he owed, then abandoned to starve.

The grandmother always spoke to her, always reminded her, "Everyone lives right next door to death, child. Trouble is most don't take the time to get even a little bit acquainted till they gotta be roommates."

And as Senga ascended the crumbling stairs of the chalky building where she rented a room, she heard the grandmother whisper now and knew it would not be long before the world remembered.

Her partner licked the air, his tongue penetrating worn wicker slats, his lungs expanding to hear the old woman's vibrations.

"Sssssssenga," he whispered, eager to curve into her warm body, "Ssssenga."

The room was dark and chilly. On the ceiling by the small railed window, a brown stain extended moist fingers towards a dim lightbulb. Senga freed her partner, kissed his flat, smooth head, then fed him fresh rats and roaches enticed out of walls.

When he was full, he twisted over her, like a colorful vine, his tongue smelling her skin, full of music.

He wanted to know something. He wanted to know. So he

wriggled up her arm like a long bracelet, perched on her shoulder, under her hair. He melted into the nape of her neck like a lover, wrapped his body once around her waist. The grandmother's breath rattled and penetrated the small, square window. Dashes of rain like splinters of broken glass chipped the cold, puckered linoleum floor. The smell of wet smoke drizzled a fine mist like a graceful genie, and the snake whispered, "What will happen? When they remember, what will happen to us?"

The lobe of Senga's ear quivered like a taut string. "Rest," she told him, "don't worry now."

PETERBOROUGH
by Derek McCormack

ASPIRATIONS

I cut corn husks. I picked hemp. I squatted by the road, smoked a corn husk dube. Stashed a spare in my silverware case.

A car. I waved it down, whipped the door open. Old coot behind the wheel. "Where you headed?" I said.

"Peterborough."

I hopped in. "Got any grub?"

He shook his head, wrassled the gear stick. Liver spots on his hands.

"Yes sir, pretty soon I'm gonna be eating caviar," I said. I knocked my case. "Once them city boys get a load of this baby I'll be set up good. Nobody's seen one of these before. Know what it is?"

The old coot shook his head. Face gray as whiskers.

"A home embalming kit," I said. "Say someone keels over, no doctor for miles. Or say you're in town and you don't wanna fork over an arm and a leg to some crepe-hanger. Know what I'm saying?"

His eyeballs bouncing: road, me, road, me.

I opened my case. Oak outside, red velvet in. I pointed to the basting pins. "For when a stiff's skin sags," I said. "Then all you gotta do is bunch it together and pin it."

I touched behind his ear. He shrank away.

I pointed to a trocar. "For draining innards. Just poke it

through the bellybutton. Makes a little fountain. Got that off a doctor. It's all rusted so he got himself a new one."

I rubbed my belly. "And it ain't right yet. I've gotta get some rubber hosing, a bottle of formaldehyde. And face paint. I've gotta get some face paint. You know stiffs wear face paint? On their lips, cheeks, everywhere."

I pulled the scalpel out. The car swerved.

"Don't panic, Pops!" I said. "You ain't dead yet!"

I laughed, shut the case. Caught some z's. Street lamps woke me. Hunger pains. On the sidewalk a fellow roasting chestnuts in an oil drum.

Pops pulled over.

I rubbed crowshit from my eyes. "Say, can you spot me two bits? I'm good for it. Soon as I show them boys my kit I'll be flush—"

"Get out," he whispered. "Please."

I climbed out, belly cramped to hell. The smell of puffed wheat breezing down from the Quaker Oats plant. I lit a dube. All down George St. folks window-shopping. A string of sausages noosed in a butcher shop. A stuffed grizzly in Lech's Furs.

VANISHING CREAM

I stalked past Gloria's Dress Shop, Peterborough Jewellers, straight into Turnbull's Department Store. Directory numbered like a phrenological head. Cosmetics-Organ of death.

Salesgirls flitting about. Fingernails scarlet. Eyelids violet. Lashes green.

I stopped one. "What's that on your mouth?"

"My lips?" she said. "That's Rachel Red Lip-Rouge by Blu-Bell. Were you looking for something for your girlfriend?"

"Do you know what's in that rouge?" I said. "Bugs. That rouge is made of carmine bugs which are from Mexico and which are dead. Dead!"

She backed away. "Security!"

"You got face cream on, too?" I said. "Know what's in it? Whale seed! You think that's decent? You think that's Christian?"

A guard grabs me. Chucks me out.

At Clark's Dry Goods I bought a tin of rat poison. I ducked back into Turnbull's. Past coffin-shaped counters. Lamps hunched like buzzards. I picked up a tester. Vanishing Cream. I shook a little poison in. Sliding down the counter I poisoned Skin Food and Skin Tonic, too.

"Stop!" The guard hollered from Hose.

I winged a jar at him. Hightailed it out the door. As I stepped off the curb a car slammed into me. For a second I heard nothing. Fluids trickling.

"Stand back!" Some guy kneeled beside me. Black suit. Straw hat fraying.

I tried to rise onto an elbow.

"I'll take care of this," he said. He pushed me down. Opened a silverware case. Pulled out a needle. He raised the thing up. Stabbed it through my stomach.

A lady shrieked. I crawled to the curb. Blood spurting from my navel, blood streaming out my nose. My spine shimmying. I lift my eyes heavenward. But the sky looked like an eye shadow sample. Black. Plum. Pink.

Evil Eye
by Ann Diamond

It began with a small wound.

I arrived early at the beach. He had his back against a rockpile. She was on a nearby boulder, reading a giant book. I greeted him in my cheerful way.

"Hello. No sharks today, I hope?"

But he ignored me. It was because of her, watching us. I didn't care. I had my swim. When I came out of the water she was being the beautiful woman, with her hair loose in the wind. As soon as she saw me she began to complain of stomach cramps.

He motioned to me with a hand.

"Be kind to her," he whispered. "My love for you is sealed by Law. But her little-girl body is endless and pure. I can't bear to see her suffer."

I had no power to stop her cramps. I offered to buy her a club soda. We sat in the little seaside café, speaking little. What was there to say? I thought of asking her, "Is this real pain you're feeling or just something brought on by jealousy? Ha ha. And why are you jealous since you are the one my husband takes to the beach? Even though he doesn't love you. You're just another of his instruments of torture. And you sense that and you're jealous of my secret. It's driving you crazy, slowly."

But I didn't say that. I'd been trained to compassion and hypocrisy. I ordered her another club soda and watched the bathers coming and going. I was thinking: she has a nose like a garden tool and what does he see in her?

We walked back to the beach, and he was there on his pile of rocks. He greeted her and ignored me but when her back was turned he gave me that look. The sun was going down in purple and red. I slipped on a rock and opened a gash in my knee and the blood dripped down. I showed it to him.

"There, you see?" But he looked away.

"It's a clean wound," he said.

My wound laughed and gnashed its teeth. "Wash your wound in the sea!" cried a voice, probably his. I waded into the brown slime. I opened my wound to the slime in which my husband condemns me to live.

And that's how it all began.

In the open-air theatre they were showing *God Forgives But I Don't* in Italian with Greek subtitles. I bought a ticket and stood to wait under an awning. I saw them swing by. She was in her pink dress and had him tucked under her arm.

They sat in the outdoor restaurant in full view of enemies and passers-by. Her hair blew in the wind and slapped against his cheek. The perfect couple—or so they thought!

Blood still dripped from my knee but now I was glad. He was staring out to sea where yachts were cavorting. I crept from the shadows and commanded my wound to open.

She noticed the blood as it crawled toward their table, up her chair leg and onto the menu. She screamed and threw down her napkin. He touched the blood thoughtfully as it travelled up his sleeve. She lay gasping on the ground like an octopus.

Sewage was collecting in the shallows. Fish were washing up, with shocked eyes, open mouths. I was zeroing in for the kill, when a siren began to whine. A little boat was approaching, filled with soldiers, rifles poised.

"We've come to clean up the beach," said the soldiers. "We have orders to rid this island of the evil eye of envy." They claimed the beach in the name of the new military government. It was the first we had heard of their little *coup d'etat*.

They aimed their guns at me. My wound gaped back. The fangs of my wound smiled.

"There's a mouth in her knee," said one.

My wound began to declaim. It spoke to them of envy guilt revenge disease and longing.

"She's a witch! Arrest her!"

The soldiers rushed forward.

"Not me," I said, and pointed at her. "She brought all this on. She's the one he disports with on the beach."

But the germs of a skin ailment entered my bloodstream. I began to glow with an eerie rash.

I prayed to God. I prayed for revenge and devastation. I asked God to drive mine enemies into the sea. I prayed for the evil eye. Winds buffeted our shore. Chips of foam struck the harbor, fish were thrown against doors and windows. The army built a radio tower to counteract what they termed a "female radiation" on our island. There were endless broadcasts. Many people phoned in and many were accused by their neighbors, exonerated by other neighbors, and re-accused. The army began to search houses for black magic paraphernalia. People fled to the mountain caves to escape the inquisition.

I hid on a secret ledge, and was much sought after by pilgrims and children. My knee continued to scream. At night it kept me awake. Witch blasphemer adulteress, it raved. I taped its mouth, I covered it up with towels. One day there were soldiers on all the goat paths. I took pains to blend in with the rocks.

I could smell the wild sage that they crushed under their hobnailed boots. The scent of their gun oil. The metallic odor of their sweat. The smell of young men in the sun.

My knee now stank, a rotting persistent hole. But for the moment it had grown inexplicably silent. I wrapped it in hot linen and hobbled to the rear of the grotto where I had taken to hiding. My little fire was out, I had no food, no telephone. Outside, the crunch-crunch of heavy soldiers' boots.

A fish came flying through the entrance of my cave. I covered my ears and crouched in a corner. A young man in blue trousers came crawling after it. His blond hair stood up straight on his forehead, like the hair of an errant goatherd, fresh and damp from a dip in the sea. There were beetles crawling round my floor. I quickly brushed them aside. I thanked him for honoring my grotto with a visit. "An interesting hole," he observed. His hand stroked the slime that dripped from the shelf of limestone where I kept my gauze and medicaments. A tin pot hung by the cooking fire. "A cozy little grotto."

"Stay for dinner," I said. "The fish is large. It's more than a single woman can handle." He had slim calves like a goat and the nicest little hooves. He took out his little pipes and played. The fish, which had seemed stone dead at first, now flopped unnaturally in the oil as it fried. I made a little salad of dandelion leaves. He ate whatever I gave him. One thing leads to another. Overcome by our meal, we tumbled into the straw.

By and by he noticed my knee.

"What's that?" he asked.

"Oh, just an old war wound," I said. "Everyone has one."

"But this one's different. It's an eloquent wound."

"Let's talk of something else," I said. "How is the war going these days?"

"The soldiers burned the pine forest on the Passa Limani side. The hillsides are covered with the skeletons of trees. Our men are discouraged for several reasons. They are barefoot; their rifles are of ancient vintage and explode in their faces. Their wives complain about the invasion and blame the Church for not putting its foot down. The priests blame the villagers. They say the war is God's judgement on the necrophiliacs and adulterers. There is a bitterness and chaos on every side. Meanwhile our own government goes on laying waste to our homeland."

"And how did you escape being inducted?" I asked. "I thought all the young men were needed in the Resistance?"

He looked away, bitter. "They don't want us boys with hooves."

Such nice hooves too. "Perhaps you should hide here for a while." I stroked his hand.

"Hide? With you in this tiny cave?" He gave it a moment's careless consideration.

"You could sleep by the fire. During the day you could shoot birds with your slingshot. I would steal vegetables from the farmers and make pies."

He shook his head. "What about my goats? How would they live without me?"

"They could live here, too."

My wound began to hum a romantic serenade.

"What's that music?" asked the boy.

"Oh, just some soldier's pocket radio."

The goat-boy began to fidget, scraping the floor with a twig.

"My place is with the animals," he said. Outside I heard his flock stirring as if they sensed his uneasiness. By dawn they had gone up the mountain and him after them, but his child was already a lightbeam in my belly.

When spring came I walked down to the port and watched the boats arrive. I looked round for a sign of my husband.

The boats tied up and the men stood around. Then the unloading began. Chairs and tables, pieces of a car, mirrors, little chesterfields. Mountains of fruit from the mainland groves. Huge cheeses like great wheels. My hand was on my belly, which was swollen out like a cheese. I looked up at the boats, their masts knocking together in the wind, the men rushing up and down gangplanks.

I felt her eyes on my back and I turned. She was there just as before, a ghost of the girl he had loved and left, thin and awkward in the spent silks of their romance. That pathetic soul. I spat at her but I don't think she saw. She just stood there, stupidly staring out to sea.

I said, "You there. You drove me to the caves. You made the soldiers come to this island. You stole my husband when it was destined that we should be together. You came between and made the wound. And now that the soldiers are everywhere, he of course is elsewhere. I hope you perceive the irony in all this."

But she wouldn't listen or couldn't hear. She blinked her eyes and looked out to sea. That's when I saw she was pathetic now, helpless and abandoned and pathetic. Even more pathetic than I was, in fact, because I had gone up to the caves with my wound and hatched a child with a goatherd. An unknown thing moving in my womb. But she'd been victorious, she'd been Queen, right till the time he'd run off. And she would never get better. I thought they might as well build a little shrine for her here because she would spend the rest of her life gazing out to sea.

"What are you looking at?" I asked.

She blinked and pointed at a ship which was entering the harbor. It flew the Star of David and drifted right up to the quay where it lurched to a halt. An old white-bearded man with a bald spot leaned over the side of the ancient ship. He lowered the anchor on a rope, by hand. Behind him, a little throng of people was doing something to the sails. Dark hairy men and little round women in T-shirts.

"What ship is this?" I asked.

She pointed to the name on the bow: *Ship of Jews*. Soldiers came running with their guns to see the spectacle of Jews disembarking. I felt a pang of horror. "Now I suppose you're going to murder those Jews."

But the soldiers laughed. "We're not Nazis," they said. "We're Greeks like you. We just came to look."

"I'm not Greek," I said. "I'm Albanian."

"Greek, Albanian," said one.

"We're all Albanians under the skin," said another.

"But this is war," I said. "People get killed in war. It's the normal course of things."

I saw them wink at each other and some smiled at me pityingly. Then I knew I'd become a madwoman during my time in the caves.

"This isn't war," said a soldier. "The war was forty years ago. Before we were even born. This is just the re-enactment. It's to ease the people's hearts and satisfy their war guilt. That's why we burned the trees. And that ship of Jews is filled with the ghosts of the holocaust. Don't they look happy?"

"They don't look happy," I said. "How could they if they're dead?"

But then I saw they did. They were staring around angelically as if stunned by the perfection of our island. A strange feeling stole over the port. Activity came to a standstill. All the villagers hurrying by seemed to stumble for an instant, and clutch at their heads. Everyone blinked as if they'd just thought of something. Some people looked at the sky. Then the moment dissolved like a bell being struck, and people resumed what they'd been doing. The donkeymen went back to shouting at their donkeys, the waiters to memorizing orders. The priest, creeping about in his dark disguise, adjusted his pillbox and straightened the bun at the back of his head. And life took up its ordinary clockwork.

Only the soldiers stood apart without a function. The talk of death and ghosts had sobered them a little. They looked at one another sadly, and someone ordered a round of drinks and some plates of the little fish fried in batter which soldiers love so dearly.

A pregnant woman is of little interest to a soldier bent on drinking himself senseless. But after a while I succeeded in getting their attention.

I asked if they had seen the father of my child.

Several laughed and said they were the father. The others erupted in songs of congratulation.

I had to shout to make myself heard over the noise of their

singing. "He's a boy called Panoyoti!" Then there was a silence. I wondered what had unnerved them all. Was it the spectacle of my belly? Or my strange, neglected look; my gray, musty rags?

I sat with them a little longer. Since I was a madwoman, it didn't matter what I did anymore or with whom I passed the time. I was interested in their theories about the war. And I wanted to see if the Jews would disembark, or remain in their old crock of a ship which loomed over the port. I wanted to see what would happen. Whether everything would begin all over, with screams and blood and massacre, or whether this was some other kind of moment, rare on earth, a moment of contemplation when history, instead of hurling itself forward with blind destructive will, instead gives birth to an interval of rest and healing. The baby moved just then and I remembered my reason for coming here this morning.

But now it seemed to me that something had slipped in the clockwork, a gap had opened, and I was sitting in the port with failed men, sad ghosts.

My mouth was dry. I asked for a glass of water.

Whatever the soldiers said, it was clear there was a war. We had shortages of everything. You saw it in people's eyes. A closed, sly, inward look. A dark mistrust. The village was ominous, hungry now. Many inhabitants had already departed, and the others were planning to slip away. Some by night, in little boats. Some on donkeyback, their belongings tied under them with rope and canvas. I couldn't blame them. I had thought of fleeing. But this war was like a dream, and where could one flee? It had happened so gently, and there was so little violence. And these soldiers —they seemed like children, as familiar to us as our own lives.

Strange to see them in their uniforms, speaking into walkie-talkies, conferring in algebraic formulas—and for what? Against what enemy? What had caused us, after all, to be invaded by our own armed forces? The military *coup* had in fact been nothing more than a polite transfer of power from one old gentleman to another. But it became an occasion to unleash the army and send it to the primitive outposts. An excuse to frighten old women and burn a few pine forests down.

Some people said that morality had improved since the invasion. Schoolboys now had models to imitate. And parents had something concrete with which to threaten their children.

When the army first arrived, it was a breath of fresh air. But in curing us of our paltry sorrows and rivalries, it created a psychic vacuum. And in that vacuum a new disease was growing. It was a sickness without a name, without symptoms. It took the form of a painlessness, an apathy. The soldiers were the first victims. They were stranded here among us; the government had forgotten them for the time being. They cleaned their guns, they worked on their posture, they gave each other shaves and manicures. They strolled here and there in disciplined groups and drove the young women wild. But they were deeply unhappy.

One of them, a boy from Crete named Apostolis, put it to me this way:

"We feel we've been let down. We can't put it into words—and anyway, that's not our job. We're soldiers, trained to fight. But we came here six months ago; we marched all over the island. We looked in all the cracks and corners from here to Passa Limani. But we can't find anybody to fight with.

"We've been trained to seek the enemy and annihilate him. But here there is no enemy. These are our own people, living ordinary, decent lives, committing small sins, of course, but that's not a soldier's business.

"So why are we here? No one tells us. Yet they speak of a great threat. We're losing our will to fight with each day that passes. Our youth trickles away like sand and nothing happens. Is it any wonder some of the men are becoming restless? They say you're a madwoman, but you have a wise face. What do you advise? Should we write a letter to our commander?"

I shrugged and looked out to sea. I took another sip of water. His speech had moved me to tears, but from what I could see there was no solution.

"Never mind," said the soldier. He eyed my swollen stomach. "Don't concern yourself with my troubles. You have enough of your own." He leaned closer and spoke in a whisper. "Tell me, what sort of child are you expecting?"

"A boy," I said, "or a girl."

"No, no. You know what I mean. People say you were raped by a goatherd. They say there was something strange about him, something not entirely human...."

"He had unusual feet," I said.

His eyes grew bright and intense. "Yes, we caught a group of them up in the hills in our first week here. Shepherds, goatherds—three or four of them. Lonely men in rough hairy costumes, wearing hats they'd stolen from women. They live like animals all year round, squatting in ruined churches, sleeping out in the open.

"They stank like animals—no, worse. Their cooking pot was filled with unappetizing sausages and entrails, boiled together. We found human hair in their pillows. They claimed to be ignorant outcasts, accidental spawn of priests and nuns. They greeted us in perfect phrasebook English. Where did they learn it? I found their presence malignant. We arrested them and seized their belongings, but they got away in the night. Perhaps we should have executed them. I still wake up screaming."

"And their feet?"

"Their feet were normal."

"Then he must not have been with them."

"Perhaps not," said the soldier, lost in his recollection. He leaned forward. "But their eyes, their eyes were not normal. Some of us believe that we were sent here to eradicate an evil force, but have been consumed by it instead."

"Deep thoughts for a soldier," I said.

"We've all begun thinking, lately," he said. "Since we realized we've been abandoned. We have to find some reason for our presence on this island. Otherwise we'll go mad. And when an army goes mad, there's no end to the madness."

I nodded. "I know what it means to be abandoned. I've been abandoned often," I said. "It's an awful feeling, worse than death."

"Is anything worse than death?" said the soldier.

"Despair is worse," I said.

"I knew you were wise," said the soldier. "Can you teach the rest of us to be as wise as you?"

I looked round at the others, absorbed in drunken conversation. They did look slightly insane. Several were gaunt and wild-eyed, talking to themselves. One was building a cockroach trap out of bits of cheese and wood, with a razor blade for a guillotine.

I thought of taking a stroll but my stomach was very heavy and my veins felt thick and clogged. It was four o'clock and the port sagged under the weight of the afternoon. The sea flashed like gold, and the little whitewashed houses shuddered in the heat. Beautiful tourists were parading almost naked, and the very air breathed out a musky fragrance. I felt I had died and was living with gods and their likenesses in a world made unbearable by Beauty. But the young soldier's tormented face reminded me of the baby, drifting inside in its human fog.

I heaved myself up from the little thatched chair and shook out the thin cloth of my dress. I leaned on the metal table for a moment. At the quay the strange ship still rocked back and forth under its ancient insignia, two triangles intertwined.

I left the soldiers sitting at their table, absorbed in the details of despair. One or two were slumped, foreheads touching the gleaming tabletop, sobbing like children. It was hard to turn away from such a scene, harder still to endure the whispers of the market crones as I negotiated a path through the square, now beginning to come alive with donkeymen and fruit vendors.

"Look at that belly," hissed one old snaggle-tooth, perched on her step at the entrance to the public toilet.

"Just wait, she'll give birth to a yellow-eyed demon!" said another. And they all shrieked with laughter.

Round the deck of the ancient ark, they were stringing up

colored lanterns, as if to salute the town. But no one ventured down the gangplank, and no one went up, either. A gentle breeze tickled the waters.

I stood in the shadow of the rocking ship, waiting for a sign. But instead, the old man came out on the deck and stared down at me kindly.

"What is the matter?" he asked.

"Sir," I said. "This is my position. It is impossible to lie. I am a figure blackened by sin and envy. I conceived a child in darkness and that child will soon be born. I conceived it in a cave and now, on the eve of its birth, something has caused me to leave the cave as if I, myself, needed something of you. I came down here to find forgiveness for myself and my goat-footed child."

The old man waved his hand. "Your husband told us to tell you he's still interested."

"Interested in what?" I asked.

"He says he is heartbroken by your desertion. He is prepared to take you back, on certain terms."

"Which terms?"

"His terms."

"Of course," I said. "As always."

"The terms are as follows: He pursues his interests. You adapt."

"Tell him I've adapted." I patted my swollen stomach.

The old man shook his head. "Your husband says this time you've gone too far in your revenge."

"Oh," I said, turning to the crowd of soldiers who had gathered to listen to this discourse. "Did you hear that? He's abandoning me! A pregnant woman! In wartime! With a wound in her knee!"

At this, the soldiers grew restless and attentive.

The old man interjected: "Your husband says your wound is not from the war. Your wound pre-dates the war. Your wound in a sense caused the war."

"But can he prove that?" I shot back.

The old man shrugged and began to weigh anchor slowly. "He says you tampered with natural law. You invoked the evil eye."

"All that's just theoretical," I said. "What about my unborn child?"

"A goat-footed child can fend for himself," said the man.

"And there's no hope for me, I suppose?"

"God's law is just," said the man. "This is your punishment. And consolation."

"In that case, I swear vengeance on God," I said, dropping to the paving stones. The soldiers raised their rifles.

"A waste of time," said the man. "God doesn't care one way or the other. He's always done what he likes. Now he's stepping out of human history. Bear children or monsters—everything's permitted now. We're sailing the seas to bring the message to all nations."

"Farewell!" cried the soldiers, waving their guns.

"Farewell! Farewell!"

I heard the rasp of the anchor being lifted on its rope. A row of faces leaned over the railing, and coins struck me on my head. It was raining coins, rare coins, too. Scooping them up, I saw they were old and irregular, imprinted with shapes of forgotten despots. There was singing from the Ship of Jews as it creaked away from the pier.

All around me, soldiers wept and tore up their uniforms.

Instructions for Navigating the Labyrinth
by Méira Cook

How do you enter the labyrinth? Reader, turn left turn left turn left.

These are the facts: the embalmed corpses of seven women their throats slit are found in a sealed basement in a house on the outskirts of the city by the mistress of the house. Her name is Annah her husband is away on business he is a traveling salesman for a company that markets razor blades and stainless steel kitchen knives. They are found at the noon hour by the wife who has disobeyed her husband: Annah beware never enter the basement never never enter the basement.

Seven women! One for every day of the week?

Everything that happens is a clue. Nothing that happens is insignificant. Not all the clues are purposeful you know. Some just sidle out—a pocket handkerchief at the scene of the crime.

More facts: Annah and her husband have been married for a full year when she makes her discovery. They live together in the house with an old family servant called Belia. Tonight is their wedding anniversary Annah's husband is expected home at seven they are going out to dinner at an expensive restaurant in the city. Afterwards, well he is a man of habit, afterwards he will pitchfork

INSTRUCTIONS

her to the bed with his iron thighs and pour himself into her creamy interiors, Annah beware never enter the basement, never never....

For a satisfying mystery mix two parts enigma to one part necessity. That is, the murderer must be known to the reader but unrecognized until one heartbeat before the moment of plot where suddenly identity must seem as familiar as idiom. It is as unsatisfactory that the murderer be outside the reader's field of reference as it would be if the murderer's identity were obvious from the first scene. This is a complicated business this contract between reader and writer in which the reader asks to be fooled but without of course appearing foolish and the writer promises to dupe without becoming at all duplicitous. An example will be given, presently.

Annah and her husband have been married for one year and it has been a good year. Possibly, quite probably, it has been the best year of Annah's twenty-five. He has been a kind husband by her lights he likes his coffee strong and his women weak. Annah buys the best Brazilian roast and grinds it herself adding chicory and lemon peel at the end. She is a splendid coffee-maker. When she went to live with him in the three-story house on the outskirts of the city that he inherited from his father, he gave Annah the keys to all the rooms.

Except one.

You know the rest.

Allez-oop!
The magician waves his hands and a colored ball disappears.
Where is the ball? Allez-oop!
Another ball disappears with a wave of his hands, they are tightly closed now, where is the ball?

In your hand, the audience roars.
Allez-oop! Another ball disappears, his hands are buttoned shut and bulge slightly.
In your hands, in your hands!
The magician opens his hands. They are empty.
(Allez-oop!)

At some point all analogies break down. This is not the point.

Long ago when Annah first went to live with her husband on the outskirts of the city, he gave her the keys of the house hung from an antique gold chatelaine. This was his wedding gift to her she has worn it about her waist for the last year because she loves her husband and tradition and the luxurious mesh of heavy gold link. There are seven silver keys hanging from her waist and they clink against each other as she walks.
clink clink clink
Annahmylove calls her husband when he hears her chains, my precious girl . . . She always obeys when he calls her because his requests are few and always just. Indeed in the past year there has only been one prohibition of any great consequence.
clink clink clink

Reader beware never enter the basement never never enter the basement!

Annah's husband—we will call him B on account of a crime that has been committed in his house and the innocents that must be protected—is leaving on a short business trip. Goodbye Annahmylove he kisses her, goodbye goodbye.

This is the example, see if you can solve this problem. Three objects lie in a field it is spring: two stones, a red scarf, a raw carrot. Something has happened some event whose genesis if only known would render each object in the narrative perfect and necessary.

INSTRUCTIONS

When her husband leaves, Annah calls Belia and together they take up all the carpets and begin to beat them. Dust flies how it flies, a good thing B is not here, Annah says, his hayfever! This is a charming fiction for of course if B were present she would hardly be beating carpets side by side with old Belia, her hair bundled in rags and her face and hands the skin he loves to touch blackened with grime. Although he does, it is true, suffer appallingly from seasonal hayfever.
Clink go the keys at her waist with each stroke of the carpetbeater, clink clink clink.
Think of it this way: if the scarf were not red, the stones not paired, the carrot not raw, think of the time the place the season . . .

After the carpets she and Belia get busy on the floors, Annah rolls her skirt above her waist so that her legs swing free. They are thick strong legs with tightly bunched muscles, they are B tells her twining them about his neck, one of her finest attributes. Annah is proud of her legs and the things they can do to B to make him forget his nice judgements his way with language. Belia glances sideways at Annah's legs but does not hitch up her skirts.

This is a clue—it is spring the snows have melted. That was a clue.

One of the things Annah has planned to do on this carbonated day at the year's hinge, the air like soda, leaves fizzing up out of bud, one of the things she must do before celebrating with her husband their first wedding anniversary, is to attend to the stuffed animals. Meanwhile she has Belia soak the crystal, polish the silver, handwash the fine bed linen. Belia works slowly with a great creaking of joints but Annah is flushed with spring cleaning, hectic with spring fever, her hair falls about her neck in damp intimate tendrils and she whistles in her pale new skin, sloughing the old one in mothballs with the winter jackets and woolen blankets. It is spring it is spring the snows have melted it is spring!

The snows have melted the rains have come (where are the snowmen of yesteryear?). Nothing remains in the gushing fields of last year's snowmen but the stones-for-eyes, the carrot-nose, the red scarf.

Along with the house and old Belia, the stuffed animals were a legacy to the young couple from Annah's father-in-law, a prodigious hunter and taxidermist of some repute whose death by his own hand, though tragic, allowed the newlyweds to live in the style to which one of them at least had never had the opportunity to become accustomed.

Question: what is the significance of the scarf being red?
Answer: red is the color of winter scarves and red herrings.

Although Annah hates to think of the small suffering creatures of this world, the blank-eyed squirrels, numb-winged geese, rabbits stunned by fear and light, the blood in the footprints of the snowfox, she is the keeper of the stuffed animals. Well they came with the house of which she is undoubtedly mistress and her attention to their well-being is in some small measure a ritual of gratitude and propitiation. But still, she avoids their empty eyes even as she brush brush brushes the gloss of their living deadfur.

This is the story of a red herring so that you will recognize one the next time it swims past.

Annah has attended to the stuffed animals.

. . . okay

Annah has seen to the cleaning of the house.

INSTRUCTIONS

>   what is green
>   can be hung on the wall
>   and whistles?

Annah is bored.
>   well what . . . ?
clink clink clink

>   a herring of course!

When Annah is bored her thoughts cluster like metal filings about the one thing she has been forbidden to think about. The basement draws her thoughts at these times like iron, the basement opens and she falls through the trapdoor skirts whirling above her head

>   a herring of course!
>   But a herring isn't green . . .

How do you enter the basement?
Walk down three flights, turn left.

>   But a herring isn't green!
>   It is if you paint it green . . .

Annahmylove beware never enter the basement never never enter the basement.

>   it is if you paint it green!
>   But a herring doesn't hang on the wall . . .

Allez-oop! This is the point where analogy breaks down allez-oop!

>   but a herring doesn't hang on the wall!
>   It does if you nail it to the wall . . .

turn left turn left turn left

       it does if you nail it to the wall!
       But a herring doesn't whistle . . .

reader, beware . . .

       but a herring doesn't whistle!
       So, okay, a herring *doesn't* whistle.

clinkclinkclinkclink

       punchline: red herrings come in assorted colors

Annah stands before the forbidden door the seventh key is in her hand click she turns the lock, click. Somewhere far overhead old Belia the maid rummages through dirty laundry and her own stale desires. Annah opens the door Annah enters the room. Somewhere far overhead another door opens a sneeze is heard Annahmylove I'm home atishoo!

       what is green, can be hung on the wall . . .

The women have the same glassy look of betrayal in their dead eyes as they swing on their hooks in the gloom of this last this forbidden room. Annah thinks of the old man who first owned the house her father-in-law, the hunter, the preserver. Annah mylove calls her husband, my precious girl . . . Of course.
Annah feels fear uncurl a hedgehog in her belly her heart sluices open strangely there is nothing of incredulity in her horror it is all all somehow familiar, appropriate even. Besides it has happened before.
Seven times already.

atishoo atishoo atishoo coming closer

INSTRUCTIONS

There is a rustle in the dark beside her, a hand pulls her into the room, shuts the door, silently, we must hide whispers old Belia, we must hide from the master. I will save you, my precious, she whispers lovingly, but Annah hears the razorblades in her voice.

These are the facts: the embalmed corpses of eight women hang in a sealed basement in a three-story house on the outskirts of the city. Once a woman called Annah lived there with her husband and an old servant named Belia. No longer. Only two people live in the big house now and it is rapidly becoming far too much work for one woman.

How do you leave the labyrinth?

Why not hire another servant, asks B.
Good help is hard to come by my love, replies Annah.

turn left turn left turn

Miasma
by Ernest Hekkanen

It started with a scent, one that wound like a bright ribbon into the dark interior of his head, then he was lifted, bodily, into the air, as though in a dream. He began to float in the direction whence the scent came, head-first, lying comfortably on his back, his nose tilted at an angle that allowed him to receive the scent as it came drifting over his right shoulder. To that extent, he was alive and in the world, for he had a physical impression of himself quaffing the odor.

I have always tried, you see, to acquaint myself with the essence of life. In that regard, I am not unlike any other writer or artist. What we hear, what we see, what we smell—these things are absorbed by us. But where do they go? Into a vast filing system? Where, exactly?

The Orphics had a word for it:—*theory*. Originally, theory meant something closer to passionate sympathetic contemplation. The idea was to enter into the object of meditation, to become familiar with its essence. You entered into a state of theory because you wanted to know something directly, without encumbrance, without the usual subject-object relationship getting in the way. That is what I aim at in my art, to get to the essence of things.

I often imagine that, on my deathbed, I will be pure sensation, all the sensory input I have accumulated up to the moment of death. What is normally outside will now be inside. It will be distilled, rarefied. I will waft about as though in a womb of sensatory memory, all confused and jumbled together, perhaps. I will sense that I am at the center of things, a kind of whirling vapor, a kind of vortex. I will no longer be able to define what is me and what isn't.

"We must go."
"Where?"
"Where we usually go at this hour."
He was hovering about two inches above the floor, staring at a pair of columns which he came to realize were the legs of a woman. Her legs disappeared up into a dress. He wanted to penetrate the darkness inside the dress, up to where the sensuous lily blossomed at the juncture of her thighs; however, she moved and the moment was lost forever. He became aware that he was floating along at her heels, staring up at a textured ceiling. Then she opened the front door. He floated through the opening, into the bright sunshine! Even the sunshine had a scent—a rich, luminous scent he couldn't quite define. He stuck out his tongue, hoping to taste it, to savor it, to know it, but it dissolved so quickly he was unable to detect the flavor.

There are three odors which I have always found irresistible. I have tried my best to analyze why they appeal to me so much. One is the scent of the earth—earth which has lain undisturbed for decades if not centuries and then is suddenly and violently torn open. The smell is lovely! It is so strong, so rich, so bracing! It's a smell which is usually hidden from us; however, it is always there, waiting to be disclosed. The second scent is that of death—a putrid, horrible odor which I have sought to acquaint myself with on more than one occasion. I have opened my nostrils wide to it, even though repulsed and sickened, because there is something to be learned from it. It imparts knowledge we wish to ignore, to flee from! The third scent I find so alluring is that of womankind. Womankind is a myriad of odors which are often disguised, often secreted away, often kept under wraps. Womankind is so redolent. Her odors are tides that ebb and flow. They change from week to week, from season to season. I crave the scent between a woman's thighs. I was brought into the world with a lasting impression of it on my flesh, one which the good nurses weren't able to wash away. I desire to be reunited with it, to become a part of it. Here I must confess a certain penchant. I love making love to women when they are menstruating. I can't get enough of that scent, which, in a way, is a combination of two other scents—that of earth and that of death. I love disengaging from a woman and finding my genitals anointed with that blood, the powerful scent of the feminine on my flesh.

Is that perverse? I don't think so, not really.

The sunshine felt warm. It agitated the molecules inside of his skin, which squeaked like that of a rubber balloon. He rose toward the sky, restrained at the back of his head by a cord which the woman unwound from a reel in her hand. He experienced a feeling of vertigo as he floated up past the chartreuse foliage of trees that flanked the street. The wind seemed to take him. He pulled against the cord, which let him out faster and faster toward that blue expanse dappled by clouds, his diaphanous skin stretching as he gained altitude, anticipating the moment when he would stretch too thin and subsequently burst.

Then, suddenly, he was pulled taut against the cord, with a firm yank that caused a stab of pain. His legs inclined at a dramatic angle, the sun bracketed by his now enormous feet.

I remember crawling through a long tunnel that some boys had dug through a hill in Southwest Wyoming. They had dug it in order to emulate their fathers, who were coal miners. I remember the tunnel pressing in around me. There was a bend that didn't allow me to glimpse the light at the far end. I remember, for a moment, getting stuck. I couldn't fathom how to twist my body and so negotiate the corner. I experienced a feeling of panic. The earth seemed to weigh on me. It had an odor—that of fear.

That feeling of fear had a lasting effect. In my early teens, I became an obsessive tunnel-digger. I dug holes in the earth, boarded them over and threw dirt down on top. I stayed underground for extended periods of time. Once in a while I would sleep there, like an animal in its burrow, in an effort to condition myself, to overcome the fear I had felt on being trapped underground in Wyoming. The burrow was dark. Dank. It smelled of must, of roots that had been chopped off and were now bleeding pitch into the dark.

Once, when I was down there, I received quite a shock. I hadn't been in the burrow in over two weeks. I put my hand on something that was cold and slimy. It was an animal that had died down there in the dark. I had detected the putrid stench on entering the burrow but had forced myself to go inside anyway. The viscous, gooey remains of the animal clung to my palm. I became quite frantic, wiping my hand off on my clothes, you know. I turned to scramble out of the burrow, but then I stopped myself, quite forcibly. I huddled in the dark, despite the horrible stench, communing with the animal that had died. You see, there was something I had to discover. That dead animal was no accident. It was there to teach me a lesson of some kind.

Later, when I went home, my mother reacted quite violently to the smell on my clothes. It repulsed her, judging from the way she screwed up her face. She sent me outside to remove my clothes. Afterward she insisted on my taking a bath in a tub of hot water generously infused with baking soda.

"My God," she railed. "I'll never understand what gets into you. The things you do, the things you get into!"

But here is the important point:—she had no idea where I had been, or what I had done; she was simply reacting, on a very subliminal level, to the scent of death clinging to her son.

He became aware that he was being towed along through the air, at the end of a cord fastened to his head, buffeted by stiff upper winds. He yearned to turn over, to look down at the earth. The sky was rather boring. Except for a few clouds here and there, it was an unremitting blue.

We live according to a myth dreamed into our flesh. For me, that myth is close to an odor. Indeed, it is the very mystery of smell. Suddenly, we are confronted by an aroma, either nice or not so nice. That aroma can inform the way we live our lives, right up to the day of our death. Really! I'm not kidding. I'm not imagining this! I'm not overstating my case!

For instance, my sister and I used to play in the feed area of the chicken house. It was a sort of foyer, separated by wire mesh from the rest of the shed. I shall never forget the smell; it is difficult to describe to anyone who hasn't smelled chicken manure treated with lime. It is a high, pungent odor. It tends to take your breath away, particularly during the summer. But my sister and I often played in the chicken-house foyer. The odor of fecal matter gathered in my psyche, stealthily, almost like a stain. Critics have made the comment that I revel in shit. Maybe they are correct. It follows me around like a companion—near at hand, always there!

My eldest daughter told me not too long ago: "You like the dark, the dark is so much a part of your life. I guess that's why I couldn't live with you after you broke up with Mother. I'm like her. I need the light. You like the darkness. You carry it around inside you."

It's odd how we communicate these things to our children.

They detect it on a subliminal level. Only later are they able to articulate it. Darkness, for me, has always had an odor. It is secretive, dank, musty. It's a chemical, furtively dancing. If you are quiet, if you are exceptionally still, you can sense it.

He floated a long time, yanked this way and that by the cord attached to his head. He became aware of a seagull circling in the sky above him and knew the beach must be nearby. The wind was stiffer now and carried the scent of a beach at low tide:—a fecund, salty, vaguely sulfurous scent that nearly overwhelmed him. By now, he had attracted the attention of quite a few seagulls. They circled, careened, shrieked in high, nasal tones, eyed him with stark, curious stares, showered him with well-aimed volleys of shit. They seemed to be daring one another to land on him. Then, finally, one did:—one perched on his knee.

As a child, I would pull my bedclothes up over my head and lie there in the dark, quaffing the odor of my flesh, trying to detect some sort of essence, slightly horrified and yet in awe. When I farted I would seal the blankets around me and breathe in the odor until I couldn't detect it any longer, trying to get acquainted with my bodily functions, so to speak. Now, of course, that practice strikes me as ludicrous, but back then, when I was a youngster, it seemed, well, metaphysical in nature. And yet, I knew absolutely nothing about metaphysics. In fact, I didn't even know the word existed.

Another seagull landed on him, then another, each one weighing him down ...

When I was around six or seven years old, I had to help my father do some plumbing. It was wintertime. A water pipe had frozen and subsequently burst. I was lying on my back in a crawl space under the house, wrapped up in a heavy coat that kept me fairly warm, a flashlight providing the only light. My role was a minor one, really. I had to hang onto the handle of a pipe wrench—to keep it from turning—while my father detached a pipe in the bathroom above me. It was dank, musty, and cold. Spider webs were draped between the joists. Some had dragged against my face upon crawling under the house. Cats had defecated just about everywhere. Little mounds with fuzzy mold on them were strewn around the ground. Then, quite suddenly, with real mental clarity, I realized that I would remember that moment for the rest of my life. How did I know this? Because of the odor. The odor! I knew that similar odors would recall my brief stay under the floorboards of the house.

I once wrote a short story called "The Mime." Eventually, it appeared in my first book, *Medieval Hour in the Author's Mind*. Basically, it's about a monk who arrives in Oasis, South Dakota. He's being pursued by a flaccid blimp which hovers above his right shoulder. The blimp resembles a moth with a human face. However, this blimp, this moth, is actually composed of innumerable flies. The flies operate in unison, because of an external force of some kind, the way cells do in the human body.

I gave a reading in Toronto a few years ago. Afterward, a member of the audience asked me if "The Mime" had a deeper meaning. I responded by saying something to this effect, "If you are true to your imagination and, furthermore, if your imagination is instructed by the fates, you are put in touch with what Carl Jung calls the collective unconscious. The collective unconscious provides all the meaning you'll ever need."

But, to tell you the truth, that story had its origins in my youth, which I only recently came to realize. On Sundays, my family didn't go to church. We butchered chickens. My father would behead them; my mother, sister, and I would pluck them. To this day, I can recall the smell of chicken feathers soaked in hot water. It was very primal; it nearly caused me to swoon. After gutting the chickens, my father would throw the innards in the chicken yard, for the laying hens to feed on. The next day I had to replenish the water in the chicken pen. I disturbed some flies gathered on a knot of entrails not completely devoured by the hens. The flies lifted all at once, scattering in all directions. But as I stood there, very still, my attention riveted on the entrails, the flies returned, alighting all at once, forming what looked like a teeming garment!

By now, so many seagulls had landed on him, he was descending rapidly toward the ground. It produced a feeling of vertigo. The seagulls were driving him earthward with a will. The force of it was palpable. Then, suddenly, he struck a large rock. The seagulls took flight, in unison, as he was torn open on barnacles and proceeded to deflate. He became a flaccid tube draped like icing over the rock. He didn't know precisely how long he lay there, but it felt like a long time. He stared at the sky, watching clouds scud across the blue expanse. Now and then a seagull would glide down and observe him rather curiously. Finally, one of the gulls landed on him. It pecked at his skin before flying off again, at the sound of a woman's voice. Presently the woman appeared in his field of vision. She stared at him lying on the rock, then, giving a little *tisk*, she picked him up by his feet and proceeded to roll him up like a towel.

Once upon a time, I lived out-of-doors—for three years! My wife was living on Mayne Island. Although I had a job in Vancouver, I camped outside in what is now Pacific Spirit Park. I think I might have been a little crazy. A little off my rocker, as they say.

One winter there was an extended freeze. It lasted for two weeks. The temperature got down to minus fifteen degrees Celsius. I remember shivering in my sleeping bag, afraid to fall soundly asleep. Had I done so, I probably would have died of hypothermia. The cold had a kind of fragrance—one of mortality.

One morning I awakened as though from a fit of delirium, remembering a dream I had had. In the dream, I had become a balloon, a human inflatable. I tried to concoct a story around the dream, but I was never satisfied with it. I didn't know where to go with it. You see, the dream was a metaphor whose meaning I had yet to unfold.

When she finished rolling him up, she carried him off to God knows where. All he could do was contemplate his own dark; it was manifold, rolled in upon itself...

When I was a little boy I used to come down with excruciating earaches. In the middle of the night, the pain would become so bad I wouldn't be able to stand it anymore. I would start to whimper, to moan. My mother would fetch me from bed and spend several hours trying to comfort me in a rocking chair. The odor of her flesh—so recently dragged from bed—was very soothing, very magical. I fell in love with her aroma. I couldn't get enough of it. There was a singing alchemy to it, which is hard to define even now.

In a way, I got addicted to my mother's scent. When my ears stopped aching, I would moan as if they did, simply so I could be held in her arms and breathe in her lovely aroma. Later, my tonsils were removed. I was taken home, but I had to go back to the hospital because I kept sucking at the sutures, causing the wounds to hemorrhage. This was during the winter. One day my sister and I were left alone in the house. My mother had to go out to get some groceries, I think. Dressed in pajamas, with nothing on my feet, I traipsed out into the snow in the front yard where I made Rorschach designs with blood sucked from the wounds at the back of my throat. The taste of the blood, the whiteness of the snow, and the spanking I got when my mother discovered what I had done, resulted in my holding a grudge against her. From that day on, I wouldn't let her kiss me. I wouldn't let her hug me. I wouldn't let her comfort me.

What odor would you call that—the odor of loss, the odor of separation? It is difficult to define; it is difficult to find a name for it, but it exists. I know it does.

He had no idea how long he lay on the shelf, rolled up, contemplating his own darkness. His mind expanded outwardly beyond its limitations, until it was the breadth of the universe—full of thoughts that might have been ethereal winds. He couldn't gather his thoughts together well enough to reach a conclusion. Too many extraneous although tangent and perhaps relevant ideas impinged upon him simultaneously, creating too many variables, and that was a kind of torment in itself. He became sentimental about the past, when the woman would inflate him with helium and take him out for a walk. Those were good days, very good ones.

Here, I am going to relate something that isn't very pleasant, so, gentle reader, if you wish to skip this passage, please do. On the other hand, what I am about to tell you will add to your understanding of this story—that is, if you choose to pursue it to the bitter end. So take your pick.

I reached the threshold of physical maturity around the time Walt Disney released the first installment of the Davy Crockett saga, the movie starring Fess Parker. All across America, grocery stores carried imitation coonskin caps. It was a status symbol for a boy to have one. The less your cap looked like a cheap imitation, the more it approached the real thing, the greater your status. From what I can remember, Theodore Bundy had one, too, one that was extremely close to the real thing—that is, if it wasn't, indeed, the real thing.

For me, it wasn't good enough simply to wear a coonskin cap. I had to pursue the entire backwoods fantasy, with a trap line and a gun. My father had an assortment of steel leg-hold traps. After a lot of nagging, I finally got him to show me how to use them. I proceeded to trap every mountain beaver in the woods. One day I took one of those poor animals to school, for show and tell. The other children were suitably impressed. I described how I was going to kill and skin it, just like Davy Crockett. Mind you, things were a lot different then. Cruelty to animals wasn't the big deal it is nowadays. What I did wasn't considered abnormal.

I belonged to a Boy Scout troop. The mothers took turns being den-mothers. On this occasion it was my mother's turn to have us boys over for a get-together. I intended to teach my fellow scouts how to kill, skin, and gut the mountain beaver I had caught down in the woods. I draped the animal over a boulder and bashed it several times with a baseball bat—just enough to dispatch it into a state of unconsciousness.

Winding wire around the rear feet, I hung it upside down from nails on the garage wall and proceeded to remove the pelt. Although terribly injured, the mountain beaver was still alive. Peeling the hide down over the body caused it to writhe in agony, but not for long. The pain caused a massive failure of some kind. I cut the hide free from around the head and held it up like a trophy—like a scalp! The other boys cheered, as boys are wont to do on such occasions. Bonding takes place around scenes of mayhem and murder. This feeling intensified when I slit open the animal's belly. My fellow Scouts pressed in close around the mountain beaver in order to touch the entrails, which go through peristaltic movements long after death.

The odor of an intestinal cavity is not unpleasant. It verges on being sweetly aromatic. Ted Bundy was there, as I have already told you. He came up to touch the entrails, too. Picking up sticks, we stabbed the body of that mountain beaver until it was little more than a mass of hanging guts and torn flesh. The intestines ruptured. Fecal matter spilled from them in the shape of gooey pellets, adding to the aroma.

Eventually, my mother discovered what was going on. She verbally abused me in front of the other boys, and that seemed to bring us to our senses. We became sheepish. We even managed to slump our shoulders, the way naughty boys are supposed to do. Later, when the episode became general knowledge, I was kicked out of the Boy Scouts—for provoking un-Scout-like behavior!

But here is the important thing. The sweetly aromatic odor of the intestines and the memory of the incident became inextricably wedded in my mind. It was an episode that shaped my life. I can only imagine how it must have shaped the lives of Theodore Bundy and the other boys.

Quite a while later, he was removed from the closet and unrolled with a violent flap.

"What's this, Mom?"

The boy flapped him up and down to shake out the wrinkles acquired during his lengthy stay in the closet. The boy held him up by the shoulders. The inflatable's head flopped backward, allowing him a good view of the woman. She was older now, in middle-age.

"Oh, that thing. I forgot I even had that."

"What is it?"

"What does it look like to you?"

The boy turned the withered inflatable around. The inflatable looked straight into the youngster's blue eyes. "It looks like a person, I guess."

"Yes, it does, doesn't it?"

"But he's made of rubber. I can stretch him. See . . ."

The inflatable was stretched this way and that, rather violently.

"Be careful you don't end up permanently stretching him out of shape."

"He's a balloon, right?"

"That's right. That's exactly what he is: a human balloon."

"Can I blow him up?"

"He's got a hole in him, if I remember correctly. But if you can find the hole and patch it up, we'll take him down to the service station and get the attendant to blow him up."

"Can I do it right now?"

"I see no reason not to, my dear."

In the spring, bracken ferns grew to amazing heights, very rapidly, creating a shoulder-high forest almost overnight. The smell was so green, so tangy! We pulled up the ferns and threw them at one another, like spears. It was a spring ritual. The ferns grew very tall and very straight. We broke them off. The green scent permeated our hands. We wiped our hands on our clothes and ended up bringing the scent home with us.

Each spring we would go down to the local swamp to catch tadpoles or frogs. Inevitably, we would fall in, more on purpose than by accident. The gray mud would coat us from head to toe, making us look like swamp creatures. The mud had a very distinctive odor—stagnant, yet teeming with life! We would walk back through the woods. Dead fir needles would cling to the mud on our clothes. We became the very essence of spring. We were part of the annual unfoldment.

The boy examined every inch of the inflatable. He pulled it taut between his fingers in order to reveal the pin-like holes.

"I found another one, Mom."

"You know what to do. Cut a patch. Apply rubber cement to both surfaces, then let it dry, then apply the patch."

"I think I've nearly got them all now."

"Good. As soon as all the holes have been taken care of, we'll go down to the service station and get him inflated."

"I can hardly wait."

"Me, too."

What am I trying to say? I think I'm trying to say this: if you trace a vapor back to its source, you will discover the dancing of molecules. You will discover the alchemy at the source of things.

For me, there is greater mystery to smell than there is to sight or sound or touch. We tend to accept, to believe what we can see or hear or feel. Such things are very tangibly there. Smells are harder to come to grips with, harder to prove the existence of. When we try to define a smell we often resort to simile. We say something smells like this or that. Then, too, there's the curious way that smells behave, the way they come and go. When we get used to a certain smell it seems to disappear. But after we take a breath of fresh air, the smell seems to return.

Smells mingle very intimately with our flesh, unlike things that are visible or audible. Smelling a fragrance can recall memories so ancient we are taken back through time to the very beginning of the universe—to the dance of molecules!

After inflating him, they slid him into the back of a station wagon. The warm interior smelled of vinyl. They drove him back to the house and there they hauled him out of the vehicle and carried him around to the backyard, where they laid him on the lawn so the boy could jump on him, causing him to bulge here and then there. He stared silently at the sky, enduring the abuse meted out to him by the youngster. Finally, the boy tired of using him in this fashion and dragged him over to a plastic wading pool. The boy tried to fold him in half in order to make him fit in the pool, but his legs kept unfolding over the side. When the youngster realized he wouldn't be able to get the human balloon to fit in the pool, he tried to submerge him in the water and keep him under. But the human inflatable kept bobbing back to the surface. When at last the boy was called into the house to have lunch, he gave the human inflatable one last kick in the ribs, then hurled him face-down in the water, allowing him a close-up view of Spider Man on the bottom.

"Nice to meet you," the human inflatable felt like saying; however, he couldn't speak. He held his breath as long as he could. Later, when the boy returned, a sudden convulsion caused him to explode. In his deflated condition, he was able to detect a certain taste in the water: that of urine and grass.

I think death will come to me when I no longer desire to smell or to dream, two activities that are inextricably wedded in my imagination.

Do you understand what I mean? I certainly hope you do, otherwise I'll have to start over from the beginning, and I'm too out of breath to do that. Really, I am.

Torch
by Thea Caplan

I am not against victim impact statements, *per se*. Giving voice to forgotten people empowers them; victims have faces, lives that were stomped. Victims addressing the court resurrect a beleaguered humanity. It restores our faith in cause-and-effect. I read the op-eds, too, and I once dated a priest. I confessed to many things I did not do then, because his absolution was so absolute, so gloriously retroactive that I believed (so desperately did I *want* to believe) that, like insurance, I was buying forgiveness for future (mis)deeds, not yet conceived. Hoarding "Get Out of Jail" cards was an alluring concept.

Next week before I'm sentenced, the judge will hear victim impact statements from the family of the woman burned in the fire that I allegedly set. I am not looking forward to this. The burned woman's mother, sister, husband, and two young boys will read prepared statements about the losses they incurred because this daughter, sister, wife, and mother can no longer do the things she used to do. When the husband states that despite the last skin graft he still cannot recognize the face of his wife, the judge, the court reporter, the bailiff, the woman's clan will be watching me, scrutinizing my every nuance. A tilt of the head—cocky; an eyelid closing—evasive, no, shifty! Was that lip quivering a twitch of pity? empathy? remorse? A twitch of guilt?

I will not be thinking such things. I know what I did and did not do, and I have made a peace, of sorts. I did not know that woman and would not have wanted her hurt. If I could control everything all the time, I would not be here. That is sure. But all this, these proceedings, the charges, even the fire, did not start on May 22, 1992, the day of a spectacular blaze on Primrose Avenue as the newspaper reported, not quite, no, it started way back, twelve, fifteen years ago, in a neighborhood a couple of miles to the north, when a young girl needed to believe in princes and patience and made some quicksand bargains with herself...

I'm debating what to do when the judge asks me, before sentencing, if I have anything to say. Of course I do, how could I not? I don't mean the usual I'm sorry business (look the husband in the eye), treachery for leniency. I mean, does the court want to know how it came to this? What *my* precedents were? Can I say to the judge, a busy fellow who enjoys a lengthy lunch, Your Honour, stretch out your legs, I'd like you to hear my story?

I'd tell him I was sitting in the breakfast nook, minding my own business, watching a gray squirrel nibble a peanut I had thrown out the window. A shadow fell over the table. A body loomed over me. My mother. She was waving a photograph, and it nicked my eye. "Look at this," she said. "And don't give me that face."

I reached for the photograph. My mother held it tight, her thumbnail moon-white and pink. We both pulled a corner. I won. It was me in the photograph—in that tacky white blouse with the Peter Pan collar. The good thing was my bra; it showed right through. My chin rested in my palm, my eyes were closed. A dessert plate with a half-eaten piece of lemon cake and a teacup were beside my other hand. I had a nifty little smile—you had to look real close, not only because the photograph was piss-poor quality—hiding in the corners, my lip curling up a wee bit, *à la* Mona Lisa. And a dreamy look on my face, like I was a zillion miles away. Aunt Sylvie hovered over me, laughing, dentures gleaming. Hard to tell if Uncle Wilf was looking at me, too, because only half his nose and part of an eye made it into the photo. Karen, my little sister, was stuffing a cookie into her open mouth. Everybody's face was blurry. I remembered the glare of the white tablecloth, hearing sounds in the distance—for a second it got quite noisy. Later that night, my cousin Rita (who had some yell) told me she screamed into my ear, and I still didn't move. I remembered the smell of sweet perfume and the skinny spirals of smoke from the Shabbat candles twisting into the air. I did not remember being photographed.

My mother's nostrils flared.

"Dad will be real unhappy," I said. "It's over-exposed."

My father was a shutter-bug. Sometimes he shot a whole roll of me, testing apertures. I'd hold up a cardboard sheet with different f stops: f2.8, f5.6, f8, f11. Dad didn't care what I looked like, but once I did a series in a Marilyn Monroe pose and he said I was a real card. Only this time there were no apertures, just me spaced-out over tea.

My mother stood over me, her face all pinched up.

"What's with you? A Shabbat dinner, and you fall asleep at the dining-room table. In front of guests! Look at you. An eleven-year-old princess. You think you're the only person in the world!" She stared down at me. I considered tossing another peanut for my squirrel. "Well, what do you have to say for yourself?"

Dad developed his photographs in the laundry room in the basement. I'd pour the developer and the fix-bath. I liked the soft red glow of the safelight, losing track of time.

Outside, the squirrel was looking up at the window. I threw him another peanut.

"Stop it. I'm talking to you!" My mother ripped the photograph out of my hand, flung it to the floor. "Why do you sleep through my dinners? And wipe that look off your face."

I said into the table, "I guess I just fall asleep." Seemed the safest thing to say.

"Why does she do this to me?" my mother said, gazing out the window. A bunch of trees stared at us. "Asleep. You just fell asleep. Is that normal to just fall asleep? After all the work I do—

you—you just fall asleep? Uncle Wilf kibitzes me, 'There she goes, off into her trance,' but he's not kibitzing. Everybody knows he's not kibitzing."

"Leave her alone." My father stood in the doorway of the kitchen. "The kid gets sleepy, that's all. Take it easy, Anna, it doesn't mean anything."

"You're always on her side. Thick as thieves, you two."

As my father turned to leave he said, "I'm going golfing."

My mother said to his back, "Easy for you, go golfing."

A few days later, I saw my mother and our next-door neighbor, Hillary Gold, talking over the back-yard fence. They wore sun dresses; my mother's had yellow and blue flowers, Hillary's was mostly white. The wind fluttered the soft cotton against their legs; they looked so young and pretty with their little waists and suntanned arms. My mother ran her fingers through her hair and I heard her say, "You *didn't!*" as if she couldn't believe what she was hearing. They clutched their stomachs, giggling, Hillary giggling! Amazing! When my mother turned around and caught me watching, she narrowed her eyes. She had me in sharp focus.

The next morning I was sitting in the kitchen listening to the Beatles on the radio when my mother walked in wearing a straw hat with a blue feather sticking up.

"Neat hat," I said.

"Glad you like it," she said, looking at the bowl of porridge she had left for me. I hadn't eaten any of it. I put a little on my spoon and rolled my tongue over the cold lumps. "Stop playing with your food. Now finish that bowl."

I hacked at a lump.

"Quit your fooling around. I'm going to hang out this wash, and when I come back there'd better be nothing left in that bowl."

"I hate porridge."

"Porridge is good for you."

She'd make me sit there until I ate the whole bowl. When she left the kitchen, I stuffed spoonfuls of porridge into the hem of the off-white curtains. I was careful to spread it because at first I'd put too much in and the curtains sagged. I dug a deep hole in the potted fern and started spooning porridge into the soil, planning to leave a little in my bowl that I could "finish" for my mother, but then I heard her flip-flops coming into the kitchen. I threw a few clumps of earth on top of the tunnel of oatmeal.

"Is that all you've eaten?"

I was afraid she'd notice the dug-up fern and the oatmeal. It looked like someone had thrown up in the plant but done a neat job. It made me think of my little sister Karen and how she did everything so quietly.

I said, "You want me to eat it and throw up, like Karen."

My mother looked at me, softened a little. "Karen doesn't throw up. What are you saying?"

"Oh, yes she does. When you go upstairs to put on your face, Karen runs into the bathroom and barfs." My mother bit her lip. I thought I had her.

"I'm not talking about Karen. I'm talking about you." She paused. "It's for your own good."

I decided I hadn't stuck the oatmeal into the curtains and fern for nothing.

My mother picked up the bowl. "Do you want to eat it or wear it?"

Very quietly, I said, "There's not much left, Mom."

She looked at the hardened lumps. Her face brightened. "Do you know what Hillary did to Paul when he wouldn't eat his scrambled eggs?" She smiled her beautiful smile. "She dumped the eggs on Paul's head. Dumped the whole plate." She looked at me closely. "Do you think Paul will eat his eggs from now on?"

I jumped up. "Let me help you," and I grabbed my bowl and dumped lumps of porridge into the sink. I quickly washed the bowl and the spoon and carefully dried them.

"Don't think you're so smart," my mother said as I ran out the back door.

* * *

The next night at dinner, I told my mother I had a stomach ache. (After school I'd pigged out on Chinese food.)

"A stomach ache," she said. "What about the poor starving children in India," and all that.

My father just kept eating his steak, and Karen was keeping a quiet eye on things.

"It's your favorite. I made your favorite!" Mom yelled.

I knew she wouldn't stop. She'd go on and on. I tuned her out. I stared into her apron, and the pockets got all fuzzy and blurred into the wall. It was more relaxing staring into the yellow tablecloth, so I stared into that.

Suddenly, everything came crashing down on my head. My hair dripped carrots, gravy clogged my nose. Steak fell from my head into my lap. My blouse, grease-stained, stuck to me like wet leaves. Wide-eyed, my mother stared at my head. My father's fork hung in mid-air. No one said anything.

My mother started screaming, "I asked her what she wanted. She wouldn't answer! You heard me." She looked at Karen, then my father. Karen didn't take her eyes off my father; she pulled back her chair as if she thought he was going to hit Mom. Dad stood up. He was still holding his fork, his knuckles wrapped white around it. For a long moment my mother and father just stood there, glaring at each other. My mother's lips twitched, and I knew she didn't know what to say.

In a quiet voice Dad said to me, "C'mon, let's get you in the shower." He pulled my arm gently and led me upstairs. My mother yelled, "Don't think I don't know about the curtains! And the fern!"

My father told me to jump into the shower, he'd wait outside. Then he said, "No, I'll wash your hair in the sink." He made a basin of hot water and shampooed my hair, massaging my scalp with his gentle fingers, making little circles, then bigger ones. I told him it felt nice. With cupfuls of warm water he rinsed my hair. "Wait," he said, and I could hear running footsteps. He came back with mother's French hair conditioner.

"Let's get rid of the frizzies," and he dumped half the bottle on my head.

"Dad!"

"Did I put too much on? Guess so," he said, flinging some of the goop into the sink. "Sorry."

"It smells nice, though. Like vanilla."

He sighed. His hands had fallen against the side of the sink. They were still. He was thinking of something else. Something that had nothing to do with me. I straightened up and waited.

My father put the shower on, tested it with his hand, and told me to give myself a good scrubbing. When I started taking off my blouse, he turned away from me, and I thought he was leaving. "Don't," I said, pulling the back of his belt. Before I climbed into the shower, he pressed a glass against my lip. "Nothing like a shot of vodka," he said. Through the shower door I could see him sitting on the toilet seat, his head in his hands.

Stepping out of the shower, I heard him say, "Where does she get her cockamamie ideas from?"

"From that loony-tunes next door," I said.

For a while things simmered down. My father would say, "Smile Period," and we all smiled. My mother played mahjong, I switched to Marlboros, and Karen and I baked brownies at night whenever we got the munchies. One Friday after school my mother marched over to the table with a plate of food.

"Tell me if it's good," she said. "It's a new recipe, I got it from Thelma, she always makes it for her in-laws and they love it . . ."

I stopped listening. "Why don't you ask Karen?" I finally said, even though I knew she was outside.

My mother stuck a fork in my hand and said, "I'm asking *you*."

It was brisket, with raisins. I looked up. She was holding

Shabbat candles. A cotton ball slid from a pin curl onto her eyelid. She knew I hated brisket, and raisins were the worst. I thought about Paul and the scrambled eggs, the steak and carrots in my hair, my father's fingers massaging my scalp. He wasn't home. I hoped we'd do some darkroom work on the weekend. I missed his cologne and his hands in the soft red light.

I swallowed a mouthful. "Divine," I said.

"Then finish it," my mother said.

The pressure cooker started howling. My mother rushed over to the stove. The noise stopped. She put the Shabbat candles into the oven to melt the bottoms.

I wanted to dump the brisket on *her* head. See the greasy raisins rolling down her cheeks. I tore the meat into threads, spread it around the plate. I'd stall, then be helpful; I'd offer to set the table, light the Shabbat candles. As my mother walked over to the table, I stabbed a hunk of meat with my fork.

"I have to go next door," she said.

"Good," I said.

She wagged her finger at me. "Let's not have a scene. I'm not in the mood."

I rested my head in the palm of my hand. I heard her flip-flops on the porch and birds chirping. I stared out the window at an elm tree until the branches and leaves blurred, everything got gobbled up. The colors ate up sounds. I hardly blinked because when I did, the lines and shapes clicked into focus. My head fell to one side. So what if my neck kinked. I imagined running through a field with a Lassie dog, the white tip of her tail bobbing in the grass. My dog would make circles and curl up in a little space she'd cleared. I'd lie down, too, my head on her warm shoulder, and we'd fall asleep.

My throat was tightening. Coughing, I hung my head out the kitchen window. The air outside was cool and light. I gulped at it. I climbed up on the radiator shelf, sitting on my knees. I felt trembling under my feet, the train. The far-off toots of the 4:52. I loved when it zoomed by, howling, filling up my head. I folded my hands on the window ledge and rested my head between the open window and the sill. I could have sat there forever, waiting for that train to blast in and out of my head.

When the train passed my house, the engineer tooted. Two quick ones, and I knew the extra toot was for me. But I didn't wave, didn't move. I slipped into thinking I was in the darkroom, waiting for my father.

My head was foggy, heavy. I forced myself to breathe, even though it killed my throat. My eyes stung. I opened the window some more and leaned out. My arms hung over the ledge, the brick rough on my palms. My arms were cold and my legs were warm. The middle of me felt nauseous. No birds. Just this hum in my head...

Pressure under my armpits. Something smooth stuck to my cheek. The air prickled my throat. My mouth wouldn't open. Something covered it. Dark melted over my eyes. A flash of light: the chrome handle of the stove. It hit me that I was being carried.

Drifting. My father's poker games, late at night, in the kitchen. The shouting, the pounding on the table, the smell of cigarette and cigar smoke seeping under my door. Me getting mad because he was with them, smoking and laughing.

A gigantic noise burst in my head. The train? It was too early for the 8:06. Cool air slapped me.

The tightness on my face lifted. My lips felt hot, dirty. I filled up with air, like a balloon. An "o," firm and warm, pressed against my mouth. I tingled. Wouldn't be Dad, he was never home during the day. Oh, I thought, that's what it's like to be kissed by a stranger. I clung to the body.

I fell into warmth. Held and rocked. I opened my eyes. A big smudgy face. Blue eyes. Bushy eyebrows. I was outside, on the grass, in a man's lap.

"She's coming to," the man said to another man in a raincoat. "You're going to be fine," he whispered, pushing my bangs off my forehead. He held his hand there. "You've had a little accident. Breathe slowly through your nose. That's it." His lips brushed my ear. I snuggled against his chest, plastic sticking to my cheek. This must be the man who kissed me.

"Is she all right?" a voice cut into my head. "Is she all right? That's my daughter!"

The man tightened his arms around me, leaving no space for that voice between us. I peeked, wanting to know how close she was. My mother's freckled knees, a broad jump away. "She's going to be fine," he said.

The man holding me was a fireman. A big beautiful fireman.

"Go 'way," I said to my mother.

She jabbed his shoulder. "What's the matter with her?"

"Nothing, ma'am. She's had a bad scare. Now why don't you go over there?" He pointed to the other side of the driveway. "Give her time to recover."

My mother stood with her mouth open. She took a step toward us. Karen, little Karen, pulled my mother's hand, trying to keep her away from me.

"Please, ma'am." His chin was warm on my forehead.

"That's my daughter!" my mother wailed. She shot me a dirty look. "What's the matter with her? Tell me. Why wouldn't she hold her breath? You told her to hold her breath, I heard you. Isn't that the normal thing to do?"

"Under severe stress people react differently," the fireman said. "Please—"

"If a fireman tells you to hold your breath, don't you hold your breath?"

"Easy now," he said, holding me tighter.

"Why wouldn't she come when I called her? I know she heard me, she *had* to have heard me."

"Why did she stay in the burning house?" Hillary's voice boomed.

Silence.

"Doesn't sound normal to me." Hillary again.

"Are you saying my child's not normal? Is that what you're saying? Is it? Is it?"

I watched the crowd melt. Evelyn blurred in with Hillary, Paul disappeared into Gertie Binstock's shoes. Mrs. Camillo seeped into the gardener's boots, and my mother vanished into the rose bush. Then I heard my fireman's voice.

"When I saw you hanging out the kitchen window I thought you were unconscious, with all that smoke. Looked like you were dreaming. Dreaming, in the middle of a fire. Dave, my partner, was waiting at the window to take you. I couldn't pry your fingers off my coat."

Here was this big important man holding me. Whispering into my hair.

"You rest a bit," he said, his sweaty hand on my forehead. I tickled the palm of his hand with my eyelashes. Slow flutters.

Hillary's voice, shrill, insistent. "How come she stayed in the kitchen, Anna? In all that smoke, Sherry just sat there?" The birds were at it again, chirping.

"They said she's okay." My mother's voice.

"She could have died in there!" Paul's high nasal voice.

"Anna, what started the fire?" Mrs. Green, curious.

I giggled. No way my mother'd admit she'd forgotten the Shabbat candles in the oven.

"I think they smashed the window." My mother, irritated. (*Cleaning up glass is the worst!* was what she was thinking.)

But I was too happy to start up. My fireman stroked my forehead with light, thoughtful strokes, like my mother did, for hours, with our cat.

"Let's get a move on!" a man's voice called out, loud.

My fireman stopped rocking me. "You'd better get ready," he said.

"Yes," I said, gripping his jacket.

His eyes were velvety and sad. Then they closed, like he was praying. I knew he wanted to take me with him.

The last moment I could feel my fireman's arms around me, I said, "My name is Sherry," but I was so hoarse he couldn't hear me.

That year I started six fires. More, actually, if you count the burning of all the photographs of me in that horrible white blouse with the Peter Pan collar. The first alarm fire (a "smudge" the firemen called it, a piddly little fire—start small, build confidence) I stuck Shabbat candles in the oven (one fireman said, "The woman's gone and done it again!"), then I got a little creative and used a propane torch on our sunroom's curling roof shingles. Did that stink! The firemen (all strangers) weren't too impressed with my renovation efforts, and one of them grumbled and said, "That's what happens when girls take Industrial Arts." The last fire of my pre-teen years—I was sitting on the sofa with a glass of vodka, and my cigarette happened to land on my mother's chartreuse cashmere sweater and poof! You'd think there'd be regulations about such things, you would not believe how fast the sweater started to smoke and the sofa, too...

I have to admit the firemen got there real quick (of course our house *was* famous). Five men—again, my fireman wasn't there. Guys with gruff voices who waved me aside, shot their water hoses at the sofa (the chartreuse sweater was long gone, just a black flaky crumple). About ten minutes later they came outside and asked me where my parents were, and I laughed because it reminded me of that sucky commercial, *"Do you know where your children are?"* and I said I didn't have the faintest idea, you know how parents are these days, and one gorilla with a mouth like the Grand Canyon said, "Listen, little lady, we got a right to know what happened here." And I said, "You and me both," knowing that vodka in a glass looks like water, and Dad would only laugh and say something like, "The kid's got taste," (he did), and later when we were alone he'd tell me how much he'd always hated that godawful pink sweater. (He said that, too.)

I walked up to the fireman in charge (the quiet one who watched everybody else) and I said, "If you leave your card I'll have my father call you." He ignored that and said he wanted to ask me a few questions and I said, "No problem," and basically I described a stupid accident: sitting on the couch, watching TV, smoking, just hanging out till everyone came home, then smelling smoke, seeing the flames, blah blah blah. Apart from leaving out some details, I didn't have to fudge much. The fireman scribbled down my statement and had this annoying habit of suddenly looking up at me to try to catch a lie in my eyes, but I played it cool, and he couldn't prove a thing. I admitted, though, that maybe I was accident-prone (it *was* their third visit to our house, best to vary the scene) because it seemed the smart thing to do, and I knew I had to give him *something*. The firemen and the truck left. I remember thinking, I'll wait a month, maybe more; I had this feeling my fireman had been called away—urgent family business, I imagined, where he was needed and relied upon.

Still, I couldn't believe that my fireman hadn't come back to our house. I knew then I should have got his full and proper name. I knew by the way he kissed my forehead he was *waiting* for me to ask. If I had asked his name, I could have found him myself, but I had been stupid, not thinking, not planning how I would see him again.

Victor, the punk next door, Hillary's other and no-good son, had been showing me new ways of starting fires (it was endless! although I was not big on chemicals, I loved, *loved*, the burst of flame on my zipper, and the warm sulfur smell, call me old-fashioned), and if I did certain things for Victor he did certain things for me, so I was pretty sure with all the action going on at my house, at his house, and other spots too, my fireman would show up, eventually. But after the firemen took off I knew I had to get myself together; I finished my drink, relaxed, caught a little TV while I could because there'd be a lot of explaining to do when my parents came home—the chartreuse sweater (a Mother's Day present from Karen and me), the sofa and all—and I'd have to listen to their harping about my carelessness, my smoking, my grades. (My mother got wound up about *everything*, one thing just snowballed into another.)

When my parents got home, the shit hit the fan. Fingering the remains of the chartreuse sweater, my mother threatened to set a match to my father's Father's Day sweater. He laughed and offered to build a fire in the fireplace and started wrapping his red cardigan around a piece of kindling. But the funniest was definitely their stunned faces when I said, "THE FIREMEN WERE HERE AGAIN!" My father looked at me with such a tumbledown face that I almost believed he was sorry for all the time he spent with his buddies, sweating on some golf course when he could have been in the darkroom with me, Marilyn Monroe. Mom flung herself on the couch, sniffing the burnt sofa, and said she was too upset to cook, and Dad said he was sick of soggy cold pizza and why didn't we go out for Chinese food, it was still too smoky anyway in the friggin' house. Karen and I coughed in agreement.

And while I was having my egg drop soup I dreamed up a magnificent torch, a fabulous fire you could see for miles, smoke billowing, flames shooting into the dark, aching for the moon, sirens wailing, fire trucks squealing, firemen scrabbling to hold on. No more measly one-alarm fires—no more bored firemen shooting off their mouths, "Just another smudge."

Hounds
by Annabel Lyon

We live in a Moorish villa next to the cemetery. We are often informed that our villa, in architectural terms, is a folly. We know this. We live here anyway. We like it.

The Boy Scouts came to the door this morning. They were collecting for a bottle drive. This took us aback momentarily as we do not have a plan in case of bottle drives. The others had seen to all that, before they left. We told them we didn't think we had any bottles. They said the previous owners always had bottles. We said we could imagine that.

The previous owners were not the builders. The previous owners were a young couple in bad trouble with each other. The third time we came with the realtor, the last time we saw them, the woman took us around the side to show us her garden and how to tend it. Here are peas and here is basil and here are red currants and here is lemon grass. The words came through her mouth like they were of her body, not some public thing anyone could take onto his tongue, anytime he wanted. We liked this about her. We squatted beside her, conscious of the tender weight of the sky.

The man came out while the realtor went over the papers. She prickled in her skin when he looked at her. She raked the earth with her clean fingers, dragging up some weedy green with ripping lace roots, setting it on the grass.

The man says, Our suitcases are packed. Our house is in boxes in trucks. You don't have to do that any more. That's their job now.

Who am I hurting? she says.

Who are you hurting? the man says. You hate this house. Excuse me, she hates this house. Are we moving because you hate this house? Are we? So will you leave it alone?

Everyone hates this house, she says. Not just I.

Go wash your hands, he says.

We keep hounds. They are lean and smooth as water, always vanishing. We whip them the frisbee out over the graveyard. They give pursuit. We are careful to play this game when there is no one around, usually early in the morning. We don't want to give offense. Once the groundskeeper was startled by a hound slipping by, slipstream in the steaming dew. He looked straight at us. Since then we run the hounds at dawn only. After five a.m. we call them in and water them and talk to them about rabbits. We put the frisbee away, and they hang their wise slender heads. How do you explain a graveyard to a hound?

The Boy Scouts are back, out of uniform. So now they are just boys. They want to know if they can play with our dog. We say, Absolutely not.

Shortly after we moved in we were told, over a pile of pumpkin in the cold farmer's market, that our house was built at the turn of the century as a mausoleum for a rich man who had made his fortune importing blue cloth, but we knew this was not the truth. The builder had been an artist named, at first, Bob Johns. He had wanted to be an architect, excelled in Arches and Acoustics, but dropped out when he failed Stress. At that time he became Truck

Stop, mixed-media artist and street performer—noodle juggler, cooked or frozen, depending on the time of year—and began to design our villa. One of his pieces sold to the Metropolitan Museum of Art for a million dollars (or whatever it took to sustain the story) and he built it. Two years later he sold it to a couple and disappeared, spooked, the realtor claims, by the peace.

The dead don't bother us.

We wanted to decorate with silk and brasses, smoking lamps, scimitar palms, and still pools. But you need women for such rooms, does with brown thighs and glimmering faces. Where do you get such women?

We settled for stars on the ceiling. We considered many different kinds of stars: Turkish, Phoenician, Lebanese. We endeavored to work within the existing structural context—we gazed around. We chose ancient Egyptian. These are five-pronged or five-spoked stars, stick-figures said to represent the souls of the lesser dead. They are simple and pretty and easy to stencil without too much dripping.

People used to like our villa.

Coming in they say, Nice stars.

We explain about the dead Egyptian stick-men. They say, Nice dogs.

We say, Not dogs. Hounds, every one. Braces and braces of them.

They say, Nice green grass. Peel-turf?

Nope, we say. Kentucky blue. This is one fast grass. Keeper mows it every morning, and still it gets five o'clock shadow. Must be the soil.

People don't visit like they used to.

We watch the Scouts from the third-floor veranda. Scouting must drain them, for they spend much of their spare time, their boy time, lying in the cemetery grasses, smoking and resting. When the keeper comes out to chase them off, we know why. Sometimes in summer, at dusk, we sit out on the stoop and watch the services at the far end of the lawn. We watch golden motes, green grass blued by the turning light. We wish the boys could see this too. We drink a drink and watch the grief and colors down at the other end. We aren't morbid. We aren't cold. We know about redemption. We have a slice of faith.

Different visitors come now. Sometimes a sister, red-gold, bringing peaches. Sometimes a mother, dark and frowning.

What is in this room? the mother says. Why are all these doors locked? What happened to that wall? Why do you need a courtyard? What is this bell doing here? When do you plan to sweep?

Lately we have noticed the groundskeeper active with a shovel. He scoops and walks over and upends in our yard. We are fairly sure this shit is not the shit of our hounds, for we are ever vigilant with the baggies, but we don't care to press the issue. We also see him smoothing the earth over the new graves, earth strangely disrupted, night after night after night.

The Scouts come to the door again, as Scouts, for another bottle drive.

We say, So soon?

They laugh, the Scouts. No bottles, Mister? Got no bottles?

We say, We got cans. Want some cans?

Sure, they say, cans for a bottle drive. Ugly house, too.

Hey, we say. This is our house. We live here.

They say, You a meat-eater?

We've stopped answering the door.

A few days later the groundskeeper comes booming and pummeling. Young man! he cries in the voice of someone's god, I have called the Pound! This shall not continue! He declaims in tones so righteous even the hounds thump their tails in approval. We sit in the innermost, windowless room, surrounded by cans, listening from afar. We think of the boys, taking their ease in the long grasses. Oh, we can deduce. And this is not about the hounds, although the boys and the keeper would have it so.

Reading the dictionary the other night, we discovered the meaning of the word "houri": a young and beautiful woman of the Muslim paradise. We want houris.

We had women here once. They all looked the same but, my god, there were hundreds of them. Plucked lips, pinked hair. In the bathroom they were slobs but some were handy, they fixed the truck and organized a recycling room. Others shouted. I'm not taking the dog out! they shouted, and, What's so wrong with the radio? Still others were quieter—they brought us coffee and spent hours carving faces into pumpkins, out of season. We made pie of the innards and roasted the big seeds with salt in the oven. Pumpkin days, pumpkin nights. But then she'd be on about the radio again, why can't we have some music, and what's so wrong with dancing now, and just who do you think will hear us, if you need it so quiet why don't you move next door? We were sad when she left but the realtor was right: some people can't take peace.

But houris. They could all look the same, and we would still want a hundred of them. We would still want every one.

We'll admit, these days, to spending a lot of time in the recycling room, with its bins and shelves and orderly can piles. We sweep it out slowly and then we sweep it out again. We pretend we are caretakers wormed into the core of some vast factory, the only slow job for miles. We pretend we are an old man and the cans are a food source everyone has forgotten but us. When they are cold and queuing, we will eat black beans and apple sauce from the flat of a knife and drink bottled water. We will sit on a stool and smoke tinned cigarettes, rub the ridges of our hound's brow and ponder lapsed time, while outside they dash and shout and overlook this secret cache of plenty, and the old bugger nursing within.

Here is a conflict. We are running out of food. We used to have pork chops in the freezer, a whole pig's worth of pork chops, and cans of mushroom soup, and some luxurious brown rice. That was a meal we were good at, but lately these things run low. We also like to mess around with canned tomatoes and tuna, garlic paste, and dried macaroni. This is another of our meals, this noodle meal. We abhor—I say, we abhor—boxes. Even the hounds' food is canned now. Three nights ago we fed them the last of the kibble. We folded the bags and bound them with twine, like newspapers, and stacked them by the back door. The hounds come sniffing, rustling the empty kibble bags with their long soft noses. Watching us with their eyes.

The city slipped a paper under the door today. The city wants the hounds. The hounds want the paper. They lick, greedy hounds; they pant and sway. Last night we saw the boys making our problems, squatting and straining, pants around their ankles, shitting on their dead. Whose children are these? we ask the hounds. What race of men produced these? They lean on their picks, long moonlit metal. They look toward us, and we believe they see. Scouts, we remind the hounds. Scouts, every one.

HOUNDS

The hounds are getting hungry. We don't know what kind of dog they are, really. We know they're awake at night, know they've been at the trash, know they've been licking at the cans, and some of them have cut their tongues. We see the blood on us when they come lapping kisses, snapping muzzles. They will blame the hounds for everything. They will blame the house. They could equally blame the Metropolitan Museum of Art or the gravity of the dead. I suppose each of us must start somewhere. But the next one who knocks, we will open. God help him we will open the door, for whatever comes next they will have asked for; and they will receive, bottles included, everything empty we own.

Contributors

André Alexis was born in Trinidad in 1957 and grew up in Canada. His collection of short stories, *Despair and Other Stories of Ottawa* (1994), was shortlisted for a Regional Commonwealth Prize. His first novel, *Childhood*, was recently published by McClelland and Stewart.

(Andrew) **Rai Berzins** lives in Toronto and writes drama for the screen. Prose fiction escapes him for the moment... though the ghost of it does not.

Thea Caplan's short stories have been widely published in literary journals and anthologies. She lives in Toronto with her husband (Tony) and collie (Pinocchio) and when not working on her novel, writes book reviews for *Event* and *The Globe and Mail*. Her collection of short fiction is seeking a publisher.

Méira Cook's novel, *The Blood Girls*, was recently published by NeWest Press. She has written two books of poetry, *A Fine Grammar of Bones* (Turnstone Press) and *Toward a Catalogue of Falling* (Brick Books).

Ann Diamond is a Montreal-based writer who has written for magazines, newspapers, radio, and theater. Her story collection, *Evil Eye*, published by Véhicule Press, won the 1994 Hugh MacLennan Fiction Award. Her most recent (unpublished) novel is *Static Control*.

Kenneth J. Emberly lives in Waterloo, Ontario. His short stories have been published in dozens of magazines and literary journals throughout the U.S., Canada, and Europe, most recently in *Antioch Review*, *Paris Transcontinental*, *Chelsea*, and *Witness*. He has also worked as an editor and journalist.

Elyse Gasco's work has appeared in many literary journals. She won the Journey Prize in 1996, and her work appeared in Oberon Press's *Coming Attractions '97*. Her first short story collection will be published by McClelland and Stewart in spring 1999. She lives in Montreal.

Kenneth J. Harvey is a novelist, poet, and essayist, and the author of ten books. His novels and short story collections have been nominated for national and international awards. He lives in Burnt Head, Newfoundland.

CONTRIBUTORS

Ernest Hekkanen is the author of thirteen books. The latest are *Those Who Eat at My Table*, *You Know Me Better Than That*, and *The House of Samsara*, the last a fictional version of his play *Beyond the Call*. Also a poet, journalist, printmaker, painter, and carver, he edits *The New Orphic Review*.

Since completing his doctorate on American Gothicist John Hawkes, **Eric Henderson** has published many scholarly articles and reviews and is working on a critical study of Edgar Allan Poe. He currently teaches English at Okanagan University College in Kelowna, B.C.

Michael Kenyon is the author of six books, most recently *Durable Tumblers*, a collection of stories, and *Twig*, a short short novel. He's forty-five and lives on North Pender Island, B.C., with, besides his partner, a dog and twelve ducks.

Annabel Lyon is a graduate of the Creative Writing Program at the University of British Columbia. Her stories have appeared in *The Malahat Review*, *The Fiddlehead*, and *The New Quarterly*, and she has a short story collection forthcoming with The Porcupine's Quill.

Derek McCormack is the author of *Dark Rides: A Novel in Stories* (Gutter Press). He has most recently completed a new novel, *Wish Book*. He lives in Toronto.

Jennifer Mitton is the author of *Fadimatu* (Goose Lane Editions), a novel set in Nigeria; *Bonjour Minuit* (Guerin), a novel in French for young adults; and *Sleeping with the Insane*, a collection of stories. She has been busy writing a new novel and bringing up a new baby, both conceived in France.

Norman Ravvin's novel, *Café des Westens*, won the Alberta Culture and Multiculturalism New Fiction Award. He recently published a collection of essays, *A House of Words: Jewish Writing, Identity, and Memory*, and a volume of stories called *Sex, Skyscrapers, and Standard Yiddish*. He teaches Creative Writing at the University of New Brunswick.

Madeline Sonik has published fiction and poetry in Canadian and American journals. She has just completed a collection of short stories, *Home Sick*, and is at work on a novel, which was recently excerpted in *Event*. She is involved in the study of magic and metaphysical experimentation and lives in Victoria, B.C.